GUN TROUBLE
IN TOWN

There was a burst of gunfire. Canavan pushed back from the table, leaped to his feet, and ran out. It looked like a holdup at the stage office.

Canavan saw Sheriff Ben Hughes come bolting out of his office. The lawman stopped at the curb and fired. Canavan couldn't see the target, only the answering flash of a gun somewhere in the street. Hughes staggered.

A dark, shadowy figure lurched across the walk some fifty feet from where Canavan was standing and suddenly pitched out from the curb and fell headlong in the gutter.

Loosening his own gun in his holster, Canavan shot a look in Hughes' direction. The sheriff was down on his hands and knees. Canavan clawed for his gun and fired twice at the shadow that ran down the street.

CANAVAN'S
TRAIL

Burt and Budd Arthur

LEISURE BOOKS ⚭ NEW YORK CITY

A LEISURE BOOK

Published by

Dorchester Publishing Co., Inc.
6 East 39th Street
New York, NY 10016

Printed in the United States of America

One

Sprawled out on the flat of his back, Canavan lay diagonally across the made-up bed in his hotel room with his big hands clasped behind his head and his booted feet resting on the uncovered floor. His gunbelt with the smoothworn butt of his Colt jutting out of the cutaway holster hung from a bedpost. His saddlebags with his hat perched on top of them occupied the room's only chair, a hard, straightbacked thing that stood next to the bureau which held an age-yellowed doily and a lamp with a turned-down light burning in it. A step or so beyond the bureau was the wash stand with its customary basin and water pitcher. A small, folded towel lay next to the pitcher. When the lamplight flickered a bit, Canavan took his gaze from the ceiling with its criss-crossing cracks and focused it on the lamp. After a moment the light steadied and burned evenly again. With a wearied sigh he hauled himself up from the bed, yawned and stretched mightily, rising up on his toes, rubbed his nose with the back of his hand and hitched up his belt. He sauntered over to the window and ran up the shade. It got away from him somehow and shot upward and flapped wildly a couple of times around the roller and, gradually slowing itself, finally stopped altogether.

Standing at the window with his thumbs hooked in his belt, his critical expression reflecting his awareness that both the upper and lower panes were dirt-smudged and rain-furrowed, he stared down moodily into the crookedly laid out street that comprised the town. There was no signpost to reveal its name to newcomers. He hadn't bothered to ask when he had ridden in at sundown, tired and hungry and anxious to sleep in a bed for a change instead of rolling up in a blanket somewhere on the hardpacked rangeland. He had seen so many towns exactly like this one that they had long begun to look alike to him. The only thing that was different about them were their names. Most of them had come into being as wayside stagecoach stations that had mushroomed into settlements and finally into full-fledged towns. There were hundreds of them throughout the west. Laid out in like fashion, all of them had narrow, planked walks, low wooden curbs and wheel-rutted gutters that rain turned into quagmires. Shabby, weatherbeaten frame buildings that were badly in need of repair and painting stood shoulder-to-shoulder on both sides of the street. Some of them sagged so because they were able to lean on one another to keep from collapsing.

As his hard eyes ranged over the street, he noticed that many of the stores had turned out their lights and shuttered their windows, leaving vast stretches of darkness that were broken only here and there by blazing lamplight that burned defiantly against the deepening darkness. There were two good-sized saloons down the street, a couple of doors apart from one another. The bright lamplight that spanned the walk and reached out to the gutter came from them. That they attracted customers and business was attested to by the solidly packed ranks of horses that were tied up at the hitch

6

rails in front of both places. Apparently too there was enough business to warrant the existence of two such establishments. Loud voices and coarse laughter and the tinkle of piano keys drifted streetward from both of them.

It was only about nine o'clock, he judged. Yet in the short span of some two and a half hours since his arrival there four times the sound of brawling had brought him to the window and on two of the four occasions gunplay had resulted. He wondered if that indicated a breakdown of the law, the presence of a cowed sheriff who made no attempt to maintain it, or if it meant that there was no sheriff. But because he had long decided to adopt a purely disinterested attitude that left no room for anyone else's problems, he gave no more thought to anything save getting himself someting to eat. He caught up his hat and brushing back his hair with one hand, clapped on the hat with the other hand. He lifted his gunbelt off the bedpost and buckled it on around him, thong-tied the holster around his right thigh and left the room. Minutes later he was striding down the street in search of a restaurant. He found one shortly. But its doors were locked and the light in the window turned out to be a night light that had been left burning. He spied a lunchroom diagonally across the way, halted briefly at the low curb to permit a mounted man to jog past, then he crossed over. But when he came up to the place and peered in through the window he saw that it too was closed. At the far rear of the lunchroom was a turned-down light similar to but not quite as bright as the one in the restaurant. Disappointedly he stepped back from the window, turned and retraced his steps across the street to the hotel and trudged up the rickety stairs to his room.

He took off his hat and laid it on top of his saddlebags. He was about to unbuckle and take off his gunbelt when he heard a muffled scream somewhere along the landing, heard a door open and heard it carom off a chair or a wall as it was flung back. He walked about halfway to his own door when he heard sobbing, then running footsteps that came toward his room. Quickly then he went on to the door and opened it. Just as he was about to poke his head out, a sobbing girl clad in a flowered kimono burst in upon him. He glimpsed an expanse of uncovered chest and the swell of firm young breasts straining against a ribboned and eyeletted camisole. Instinctively he put out his hands to ward her off. But she broke through them and thumped against his body and even though he curled his big hands around her arms to push her away, she managed to withstand them. There were uneven bootsteps outside and a burly man with a mop of mussed hair, beady, bloodshot eyes and a growth of black, stubbly beard on his pock-marked face lurched into the doorway. He swayed a little from side to side. Saliva oozed out of a corner of his mouth; he wiped it away with the soiled, turnedback cuff of his undershirt sleeve. He thrust out a hairy, thickwristed and dirty fingernailed hand for the girl.

"All right, you," he said gruffly to Canavan. "Leggo o' her. She belongs to me."

The girl broke away from Canavan, easily avoided the burly man's lunge for her, and whirled around behind Canavan.

"I don't belong to him or anyone else," she cried. "I was in my room changing my dress when I happened to turn around and saw him standing in the doorway. How he got in without me hearing him, I don't know. The way he gaped at me, that—that filthy beast!"

"Lousy young trollop," the man said darkly. "You

8

go callin' me names and I'll slap your ears off.'' Then he said to Canavan: "Her boss said he'd fixed it up for me with her. He must've because she left the door open for me. But soon's she saw me, she put up a holler." Then again to the girl: "Come on, I said. You got my dough. Now I aim to get what I paid for."

"I don't want your money," she cried at him. "It's where you put it. On the bureau. Go and get it and go back to Rogers and tell him if he thinks he owns me, I don't want to work for him any longer."

The stubbly-faced man lurched across the threshold. He stopped instantly, a little unsteadily though, when Canavan moved in front of him, barring his way.

"Oh," he said. "So that's the way it's gonna be, huh?"

"That's right," Canavan told him evenly. "This is my room and I don't want you stinkin' it up for me. So you'd better haul yourself outta here."

The burly man glared at him for a long moment. Then he pulled back his right fist. But Canavan who was watching him alertly was ready for him when he swung. He blocked the rather clumsily and wildly thrown punch with his left arm and exploded his own right fist squarely in the middle of the bristly face. The full power of Canavan's muscular two-hundred-pound body was behind the pulverizing blow. It sent the man careening backward out of the room. His buckling legs carried him across the narrow landing. He crashed into the banister rail. It splintered under the impact. But it held though. Canvan heard the girl gasp when the man toppled over the rail and plummeted downward and disappeared from sight. An instant later Canavan heard his body thump on the stairs, heard him cry out as he rolled down the few remaining steps to the bottom. Bolting out of the room and peering down over the rail,

Canavan saw the man drag himself up to his feet, and clutching his right arm to him with his left, stumble out.

Slowly Canavan turned around. Holding her kimono tightly in place around her, the girl was still standing where she had been before. Their eyes met. As he halted in the open doorway, he said: "You can go back to your room now. I don't think he'll be around again to bother you. Leastways not for a while. Way he was holding his arm when he staggered out, I kinda think he musta broken it."

"I don't know what I would have done if it hadn't been for you."

He made no response to that.

"I don't even know your name," she said.

"Does it matter? Chances are we'll never see each other again."

"Mean you're leaving town?"

"At dawn tomorrow."

"Going home?"

He shook his head. "Wherever I hang my hat is home."

"Oh!" she said.

"I'm heading for California."

"I've heard it's beautiful country out there."

"It is."

"Then you've been there before?"

He nodded and she said wistfully: "Wish I were going there."

"What's to stop you?" he countered. "The stage'll take you to the railroad and you c'n go the rest o' the way by train."

"That the way you're going?"

"No. I'm going the cheap way. On my horse. It'll take me a mite longer that way. But that's all right. California'll still be there."

"Wonder how much it would cost me by stage and train?"

"Haven't any idea."

"I was just wondering. No more than that though because whatever it would cost, it'd be more than I can afford. So I guess California's out for me," she said with sudden bitterness. Then with startling suddenness her tone and manner changed. She smiled, and her rouged, parted lips revealed clean, white, and even teeth, and she went on, "Maybe one 'o these days when I've had my fill of this flea-bitten town, I'll point myself westward and start walking. And like you, it won't matter any how long it takes me to get where I'm headed. Just so long as I get there."

"Hope you're good at walking," he remarked with a smile.

They stood facing each other in silence after that, each eyeing and appraising the other. He had already taken note of the fact that she was pretty. She was about twenty-three, he judged. While he wondered how long she had been working in a saloon, he decided that it wasn't exactly new to her. It was a tough life, and the recognizable signs of her calling were there. There was a bold, challenging, tempting look in her eyes, and a studied and deliberate sensuous way in which she held her kimono around her. It accentuated every curve in her body. Then too she had learned how to stand in front of a man, thrusting out her breasts in order to whet his appetite for her. And finally, the cheap rouge that she used so lavishly on her cheeks had already begun to take its effect. It left tiny pinpoint holes in the skin. Perhaps the average man might not have noticed. But Canavan did. He had seen so many others like her in his long years of knocking around the cattle country that there was no need for her to tell him anything about herself.

11

In turn she found herself eyeing him interestedly. He was a big man, an inch or two over six feet, she told herself. Actually he was taller than that, six feet four. His shoulders were broad and he was as flat-bellied as a boy. Big men, she knew, tended to put on weight around their stomachs once they lost their youth. But he hadn't. He would prove to be the exception, she decided. She had already taken approving notice of his red hair, and more particularly, of his even features. He was not handsome. But he was good looking in a man's way, and she liked what she saw. And the manner in which he had handled and disposed of the burly, dirty-looking man who had slipped into her room impressed her. She hadn't met many like Canavan—in fact very few, and it made her wonder. When her curiosity overcame her, she asked: "You a lawman, a marshal or something?"

"What made you think that?"

"Well, are you or aren't you?"

"I was a Texas Ranger for about nine years."

"I thought so," she said. "There's something about you, the mark of a lawman on you."

"Mean it stands out on me?"

"Only in the way you handle yourself. You have confidence, and you know how to use your fists. That comes from experience, doesn't it?"

"I suppose so."

He backed out of the doorway to permit her to pass. She flashed him a smile as she glided out.

"Bye," she said over her shoulder. "And thanks again."

"Bye," he responded. "Good luck."

She halted briefly and looked back at him. "Thanks," she acknowledged. "I'll need it."

He followed her with his eyes. When she reached her room, three doors up the landing from his and the one

12

nearest the stairs, she went in and closed the door behind her. He stood motionlessly, listening, waiting to hear the key turn in the lock. When he heard her lock the door, he stepped into his own room and swung the door shut.

As he unbuckled his gunbelt, he thought to himself: "Wouldn't've had to ask her twice to come along with me. Bet she'da taken me up on it right off. And that woulda been all I need, to tie up with somebody like her. That wouldn't be just asking for trouble. Woulda been beggin' for it."

He was up at five the next morning. With his saddlebags riding across his left shoulder and his rifle, reclaimed from under the bed, clutched in his right hand, he emerged from the hotel and stood for a while on the walk fronting it and ranged his critical gaze over the deserted street. In the thin pre-dawn light the town looked its shabbiest. He sauntered across the street. He was waiting in front of the lunchroom when its proprietor, a lean, round-shouldered and tired-looking man in his late forties or early fifties, appeared.

He eyed Canavan almost respectfully, and asked a little grumpily: "S'matter, mister? Don't you like to sleep?"

"Sure. But when I'm hungry I want to eat."

The man grunted, unlocked the door and led the way inside. He headed for the rear and disappeared briefly. When he reappeared some minutes later he had removed his hat and coat and had donned a long, soiled apron that flapped around his ankles. Canavan had draped his saddlebags over a stool at the counter and was straddling the one next to it with his rifle propped up between the two stools and leaning against the counter.

"Coffee'll be ready in about ten minutes," the proprietor announced. "What d'you wanna eat?"

13

"Double order o' hot cakes, some bacon an' coffee."

"Comin' up."

Canavan eyed the man. "You mad at something," he asked, "or is that the way you always look?"

"What's there to be bright an' cheerful about?" the lunchroom owner demanded. "Lousy, two-bit town, I wish t'hell I could clear outta here and go somewhere's else. Only that takes dough and I don't have it. Leastways not enough for what I'd like to do. So with nothing to look forward to, what's there to be bright an' chipper about?"

Canavan had no ready answer for him. The man turned and trudged away, pushed through a swinging half-door that led to the kitchen.

For a time Canavan sat hunched over the edge of the counter on his folded arms. When he heard the approaching crunch of wagon wheels and the dull clop of horses' hoofs, he turned his head and looked out to the street and saw the early morning stage come rumbling into view and brake to a stop in front of the hotel. He got up from his stool and stood in the doorway, saw the driver climb down from his high seat and tramp inside. After a couple of minutes Canavan retraced his steps to his stool and straddled it again. Time passed. When he began to get impatient, he jerked around toward the kitchen, and just as he was about to call out and ask how his breakfast was coming along, the proprietor emerged, backing out through the swinging door, and brought him a heaped up plate of hot cakes and a smaller plateful of crisp, sizzling bacon, and put them down in front of him.

"Ah," Canavan said, moving in a little closer to the counter. "Looks good and smells even better."

Tarnished silverware was forthcoming as was a cup of steaming hot coffee.

"Sugar an' milk?"

"Nope," Canavan replied. "Like my coffee just the way it is. What time's that general store open?"

"Oughta be open now."

Even though Canavan didn't ask him to do it, the disgruntled man tramped to the window, and craning his neck, peered downstreet.

"Yeah, she's open," he announced as he turned around.

Some fifteen minutes later Canavan left the lunchroom, crossed the street, and marched past the general store and turned down the alley that led to the stable. When he reappeared shortly after he was leading his saddled horse, a sleek and light-footed mare whose previous owner had misnamed her Willie. His blanket roll that he had left in the stable was strapped on behind the saddle. His rifle was pushed down into the boot while his saddlebags were slung over the mare's back. Up the street they went. Halting in front of the general store, Canavan tied Willie to the hitch rail, and stepping up on the walk, crossed it and went inside. When he came out again he had a small but well-filled gunny sack with a drawstring at the top of it riding his shoulder. Willie eyed the sack wonderingly, perhaps with some misgivings too, when Canavan hung it from the horn. He climbed up on her, backed her away from the rail, and shifting himself into a somewhat more comfortable position in the saddle, rode up the street. As he neared the hotel he noticed that the stage had gone. He noticed too that the town had finally awakened from its sleep, and was preparing to face the new day. Evidence of it was the appearance of several of the townspeople, a handful of men who were going to work, and a couple of women with marketing baskets clutched in their hands. The men glanced at him as he came abreast of them. The women did not. Willie quickened her pace of her own accord and began to lope. A couple of times she

15

looked around at the gunny sack that was thumping against her side, and snorted, voicing her disapproval of it. But Canavan ignored her. So grumbling deep down in her throat she loped on.

They were nearing the corner with the open road ahead of them when a rifle cracked spitefully, startling the mare. A bullet whined past her head and tore into the wooden curb beyond her. Instantly Canavan twisted around, his gun flashing in his hand at the same time, seeking the rifleman. He caught a glimpse of a rifle barrel poked out at him from an alley. Then he spotted a burly figure with a heavily bandaged right arm peer out at him and he knew the identity of his assailant. He pegged a shot at the man. The bullet struck the far side wall of a frame building that flanked the alley and must have spewed gouged-out splinters at the rifleman forcing him to beat a hasty retreat for now there was no sign of him. When Canavan jerked the reins, the mare bounded away with him. Moments later they had left the town behind them and were racing away westwardly over the open road that spread away before them. Pulling up and bringing the mare to a stiff-legged, sliding stop, Canavan looked back. The burly man was standing on the walk with his lowered rifle in his left hand, and like some passersby who had stopped and turned around to follow his gaze, looked long and hard at Canavan who was not out of rifle range. Squaring around and holstering his gun, Canavan nudged Willie with his knees and the mare trotted away only to break into a lope almost immediately afterward. But when she again sought to quicken her pace, Canavan pulled back on the reins, slowing her. She snorted protestingly and fought for her head. When Canavan refused to ease up on the reins, she renewed her deep-throated grumbling. When he reached down and patted her, she stopped her grumbling and whinnied happily and loped along.

16

Two

Following the freshly cut wheel ruts, Canavan knew that the stage couldn't have gotten too far ahead of him even though it had pulled out probably some twenty minutes before he had. So he expected to sight it shortly. He spotted it suddenly, sooner than he had expected, when he rounded a bend in the road. Drumming along at a steady pace, the loping mare gradually narrowed the distance between them, a little more than half a mile, Canavan judged. Willie finally overtook the lumbering vehicle, came up behind it and swerved around it in order to pass it. As they came abreast of it, a woman's rouged face appeared at one of the open windows.

She smiled and called out cheerily: "Hey, Ranger!"

Canavan recognized her at once. It was the girl from the saloon. He grinned back at her and waved his hand, rode past her, exchanged a half-salute with the driver, forged ahead of the stage and pulled into the middle of the road. Even though the girl meant nothing to him it was only natural that her unexpected appearance should make him wonder about her.

"Last night she didn't have the dough," he thought aloud to himself. "But this morning she's got it. Wonder if she had to roll some drunk in order to swing

17

the trip. Wouldn't put it past her.''

He gave no further thought to her. Willie had already begun to increase the distance between the stage and themselves. The miles continued to fall away behind them. At noon he pulled off the road, guided the mare up a slight embankment, halted her when he came upon a good spot for a fire and swung down from her. Minutes later he was boiling water for coffee. He munched three biscuits of a good-sized bagful that he had bought at the general store and washed them down with two cups of coffee.

He was just about to mount and resume his journey when the stage came rumbling up into view. He waited at the side of the road till it came up to him, and again the girl and he waved to each other. Again he followed the stage. This time though he held the mare down, refusing to let her put on a spurt and get ahead of it. When the mare took to grumbling, he spoke sharply to her and she subsided.

Throughout the long afternoon Canavan permitted the stage to lead the way. Then at about five o'clock when the long-fingered shadows of approaching evening began to reach out over the land and drape a filmy veil over it, there was a sudden crash ahead of him. He looked up instantly. The stage had toppled over and lay on its side with its free wheels still spinning.

He lashed Willie with the loose ends of the reins and sent her pounding up the road. He brought her to a sliding stop at the side of the stage and flung himself off the quivering mare. The stage's right front wheel had come off somehow, plunging the top-heavy vehicle to the ground. Canavan spotted the wheel; it had rolled across the roadway and caromed off some thick brush that flanked the road and toppled over. The four horses that had been hauling the stage were still standing in the traces, their sides heaving and their eyes ranging about wonderingly. One of them whinnied when he saw Canavan. But the latter ignored him. He was concerned only for the girl.

He scurried around the stage to the other side of it, yanked the door open and peered inside. She lay on her knees in a huddled, doubled-over position with her head bowed against the far side door. He reached in, got his arms under her and carefully lifted her out. There was no blood on her face, so he decided that she had struck her head on something and had been knocked unconscious.

Turning with her in his arms, he carried her off to the side of the road, knelt down with her and gently eased her down into the thin grass that carpeted the area. Quickly he returned to Willie, dug in his saddlebags for his canteen, opened it as he hurried back to the girl, and wetting his bandana, swabbed her face and pressed the bandana to her wrists, eased back on his haunches and peered closely at her.

When she moaned and stirred, he was relieved. When she opened her eyes and focused them on him, he said: "Don't move. Stay put while I go see about the driver."

He came back to her after a couple of minutes and bent over her again. Her eyes held on him and probed his grim face.

"He all right?" she asked him.

"He's dead," he told her simply and she caught her breath. "Broke his neck," he added. "Now what about you? Anything hurt you?"

"My head," she replied, and raised her right hand to her head and touched it gingerly. When he bent closer over her and used his big fingers to part her hair over the spot she had indicated, she asked: "See anything there? Any blood?"

"No," he said. "Just a good-sized bump. Musta hit your head on the door or maybe on the roof and knocked yourself out. But you'll be all right."

"That's nice," she said a little sarcastically, and demanded: "What am I supposed to do now? Just wait around for another stage to come along? Suppose it doesn't show up for say a couple o' days? They'll find me laying here with a bump on my head and the rest o' me dead of starvation."

"Don't go getting ahead o' yourself," he said. "Gimme a chance to think and figure out what to do with you."

Her eyes burned.

"While you're doing your thinking, how about getting me up on my feet? Or will that interfere with your thinking?"

He ignored her sarcasm. "Have anything to eat today aside from your breakfast," he asked.

"Didn't have any breakfast," she answered crossly. "There wasn't enough time."

"Then the first thing I'd better do is fix you something to eat."

"Yeah? Like what?"

He frowned, his expression reflecting his annoyance with her. He made no attempt to conceal his feelings when he said curtly: "I don't haul a restaurant around with me. So you won't be getting steak with all the trimmings. You'll have to be satisfied with what I've got."

"All right," she shot back at him. "No reason for you to act up with me. I didn't ask for this to happen. When you get right down to it, if you hadn'ta got me all worked up about California, I supposed I'da beefed some but I still woulda been satisfied to stay put where I was and with what I had going for me. So you see,

20

you're really to blame for this."

"I am, huh?"

"'Course. What's more, Mister Whatever-your-name-is—"

"You talk too much," he said, stopping her with an impatient gesture. "So for a change, I think you'd better listen and listen good. You've got a temper and a nasty tongue, and I don't like either o' them. Even so I'm willing to do what I can for you because you're in a bad spot. But I'd do the same for anybody, even a dog. You keep runnin' off at the mouth with me and I'll leave you flat. So you'd better watch it."

She made no reply. He got his hands under her armpits and sat her up.

"How's that?" he asked her. "All right?"

"Yes. But I'm a little woozy though," she said, curling her hands around his wrists and clinging to him.

"Think maybe you oughta lay back awhile longer?"

"No. I'd rather sit up. You go ahead with what you were going to do." She took her hands from his wrists. As he stood up, she asked: "Got a bottle with you? I could do with a shot."

"'Fraid you'll have to do without it."

"Thought every man carried a bottle in his saddlebag. But you have to be the exception. You have to be different. Figures though, doesn't it, that it'd be your kind that I'd get mixed up with? Funny though. Thought I had you figured back there in the hotel. Guess I was all wrong about you. Maybe that happened because I've never had 'ny dealings with characters like you."

"That makes us even. I've never had 'ny dealings with steerers and drunk rollers. Although I've seen enough o' them in my travels. But they don't rate very high in my book. So I've steered clear o' them. Last night you said you didn't have enough dough to carry

21

you all the way out to California. But alluva sudden you're in the chips. What'd you do, roll some drunk after you went back to work?''

Her eyes blazed. "None o' your damned business!" she flung back at him.

He turned on his heel and strode away. She followed him with narrowed, angry eyes. She watched him set to work building a fire. He returned to the idling mare to haul the coffeepot and a small frying pan out of his saddlebag and dig in the gunny sack for a couple of paper-wrapped things. He knelt on one knee, his back turned to her, as he worked over the fire. When the fragrance of freshly brewed coffee reached her, she raised her head and breathed it in.

When she smelled the panful of bacon that he was frying, she forgot she was angry with him, and called out: "That smells awf'lly good!"

He looked around at her over his shoulder. "Then you won't mind that it isn't steak?''

"I won't mind at all!''

Minutes later he brought her a tin plate that was covered with criss-crossed strips of sizzling bacon, two biscuits that he had warmed up for her, and a cup of coffee.

"Sorry, but I don't have any tools. Think you can manage with your fingers?''

"Oh, sure!''

He squatted down in the grass opposite her and watched her eat. She looked up when she felt his eyes on her and said: "You're quite a hand with a skillet. And this bacon is out o' this world." She lifted the tin coffee-cup and sipped some of its contents. "Where'd you learn to make coffee like this?'' she asked.

"From a Chinam'n," he told her.

"He must've been quite a cook."

22

"He was."

"Aren't you going to eat?"

"Yeah, sure. Just waited to see that you were makin' out all right."

"I'm making out just fine."

He got to his feet, turned and marched back to the fire. He rejoined her shortly with another tin plate of bacon and a cup of coffee for himself, eased himself down again and sat crosslegged in the same place he had occupied before.

She watched him eat for a while, then she said: "Something I want to tell you."

"Why? You don't have to, you know. You don't have to account to me for anything."

"I know. But I want you to know this anyway."

"All right. If it's that important to you."

"I didn't roll anybody last night. When I told Rogers that I was quitting and heading for California, he surprised me by paying for the whole week even though there were still three days to go. Then on top o' that, he threw in an extra ten spot. That's how I was able to swing the stage fare."

"Uh-huh," he said.

"I figured I'd take the stage to Hopewell, the county seat. The railroad comes through there," she continued. "Get me a job in one of the saloons and stay put there for a couple o' weeks or even a little longer, all depending on how much I'm able to put away. Once I've got me some kind of a stake, I'll quit and take the train west."

He made no response to that.

"I wanted you to know," she said simply, "so you wouldn't go on thinking the worst of me."

He nodded and asked: "Have enough, or d'you want some more?"

"I wouldn't know where to put any more. I ate like this was my last meal."

"How's your head feel?"

"Still hurts. But I feel better here," and she indicated her stomach. "So I guess I'll live."

He removed the tinware. She saw him rinse out the coffeepot and wash out the frying pan, the plates and the cups, dry them with a piece of striped cloth that she decided must have been part of a shirt, and stow them away in one of his saddlebags. He stamped out the fire and kicked dirt over it, smothering it completely. He disappeared briefly around the front of the stage, backed the horses out of the traces and tied all four of them to the rear wheel. He led Willie a little inland from the road and tied her up behind some of the brush, unstrapped his blanket roll and yanked his rifle out of the saddleboot and carried them away with him. He found a spot that was fairly thickly grassed, flipped open the blanket and spread it out and laid his rifle in the middle of it. He trudged back to the stage, rummaged around inside of it and backed away from it with a folded sheet of canvas and a lantern. He made a light in the lantern. The darkness had settled over the land and the lantern, swinging from his hand, burned yellowishly against the night.

He put down the lantern in front of the girl, knelt and helped her to her feet. She bowed her head against his chest for a moment or so.

"Think you can make it over to the blanket?" he asked.

"I—I don't know. I'm a little dizzy. But I'm willing to try if you'll stay close to me."

"No, no sense to that," he said, handing her the lantern. "Hang on to it so I c'n see where I'm going."

He lifted her in his arms and carried her over to where

24

he had spread out the blanket, knelt with her in about the middle of it and gently eased her down.

"Lay back," he instructed her, and she obeyed.

He fumbled around till he found the low-knotted ends of the laces of her high shoes. "You don't have to do that," she said, but he proceeded to unlace and remove her shoes.

He reached across her and drew the other half of the blanket over her, and said: "Sleepin' out in the open can't begin to compare with sleepin' in a bed. But when you can't have a bed, you have to settle for the next best thing." She made no reply and he went on. "I know it's kinda early for you to be turnin' in. But you oughta be tired enough to sleep anyway. So give it a try."

He climbed to his feet, caught up the lantern and marched off with it. She followed him with her eyes. The distorting night light made him look even taller and more broad-shouldered than he was. When he disappeared in the darkness, she slumped down again. It was ridiculous, she thought to herself. She would never tell it to anyone because she knew she wouldn't be believed. He had come to her assistance the night before, and now he was taking care of her even to the point of taking off her shoes. Yet neither of them knew the other's name. And when he finished whatever he had gone off to do, she was sure that he intended to get in under the blanket with her. Up since dawn, it had been a long and tiring day for her. In addition the blow that she had received made her head throb. It subsided only when she closed her eyes. But because she was determined to stay awake, she opened them again. Despite her resolve, the steadily deepening darkness and the silence that had draped itself over the open countryside proved overpowering and she surrendered to them, closed her eyes and fell asleep. Proof of her weariness was the deep sigh that came from her.

She awoke with a start when there was movement close by her and she heard something heavy drop in the grass. She raised up again when she saw a tall figure that she recognized. "Oh!"

"I wake you up?" Canavan asked.

"It's all right," she assured him. "I was only dozing."

"So used to being alone, 'fraid I forgot you were here and dumped my saddle without thinking. I'm sorry."

"Forget it. Oh, meant to ask you this before. What'd you do about the driver? Leave him laying out there in the road?"

"No. Found the lantern and some canvas under the seat inside the stage and rolled him up in the tarp and laid him in the grass at the side o' the road."

She couldn't see the light from the lantern and took that to mean that he had blown it out. He seated himself on the blanket and tugged at his boots and finally got them off, lifted the blanket and drew it up over him, and turned himself on his side with his back to her.

"If I snore," he said over his shoulder, "just give me a poke. G'night."

"G'night," she responded.

She lay rigidly for a while, refusing to doze off again till she was certain that he was asleep. A couple of times she felt herself dropping off and doggedly forced herself to stay awake. She turned toward him and looked in his direction, raising herself up on her elbow to peer at him. He appeared to have fallen asleep but she couldn't tell for certain even though she could hear his measured breathing. She found herself wondering about him, wondered what he was really like, wondered if he had ever been married, and if he had, what kind of a woman he had chosen for his wife, and finally what had become of her that had turned him into a footloose wanderer.

Remembering what he had said about steerers and drunk rollers, she smiled a little scornfully to answer, and thought: "Maybe she wasn't as straight-laced as he was and when she couldn't stand him any longer, walked out on him. Maybe that soured him on all women and explains why he's footloose. Wonder if that's it?"

He stirred once and she stopped her conjecturing and held her gaze on him. But then he lay quietly. Sleep overtook her again shortly after that.

It was morning when she awoke, again with a start. It took her a minute to remember where she was and how she had gotten there. Then she saw that she was alone. The blanket had been drawn up closer around her. She couldn't recall having done that, and decided that he had done it when he had awakened. There was an uncomfortable chill in the air despite a warming sun overhead. She forced herself up into a sitting position and hastily made a grab for the blanket and pulled it up around her and huddled in it. She was agreeably surprised to find that movement of her head did not cause it to throb. She raised her eyes when a tall figure topped the tiny upgrade that led inland from the road. As he neared her she saw that he was carrying a cup of coffee.

"Think this oughta help you stand the chill," he said and handed it to her.

She sipped it and looked up again.

"Good and hot," she said. "I can feel it all the way down to my toes. Thanks."

"Just a part o' the service."

"You keep it up and you'll spoil me for sure."

He smiled. "Sleep all right?"

"Woke up a couple o' times," she replied. "But went right back to sleep each time. So all in all, I'd say I had a pretty good night."

"Take your time with that coffee. I've got some

things to do," he said and turned to go but stopped and looked back at her and asked: "How's your head feel?"

"All right."

"No more dizziness?"

"No sign of it so far."

"Good," he said, and tramped away.

Minutes later when he rejoined her he found her on her feet, looking down at herself critically. Her dress was badly wrinkled and so was the short jacket she wore over it. She raised her eyes to meet his.

"I'm a mess," she said unhappily. "I feel like one and I'm sure I look like one."

"I wouldn't say that. Outside o' lookin' a little wrinkled and your hair needing a mite o' fixing, I think you look fine. Oh, that box that got dumped off the top o' the stage, one made outta some kind o' cloth with flowers in it, that yours?"

"Yes. My clothes are in it."

"Want it?"

"Please. I'd like to change into another dress."

"I'll get it for you. When you're ready to have your breakfast, lemme know."

She had changed her dress and combed her hair and had even rouged her face and lips and applied cologne. When she came close to Canavan, he made a wry face.

"What's the matter?" she wanted to know.

"You have to use all that stuff even when you aren't working? Y'know you were in my room only about ten minutes. But when I got up this morning I could still smell that—that cologne. And that stuff you use on your face, don't you know what it's doin' to your skin?"

She looked annoyed.

"It's a good thing I'm not married to you," she retorted.

"You c'n say that again."

"You'd have me looking like an old frump."

"You've got a nice face. So why d'you have to use all that paint and make yourself look like a Comanche on the warpath and smell like his squaw?"

Tight-lipped, with her eyes burning, she said angrily: "Why don't you leave me here and go on your way? Maybe the next man who comes along won't be so fussy when he sees and smells me? Maybe he'll like me just the way I am? I've known a lot of men who've liked me and who would've taken me in a minute."

"I wouldn't do that to a dog," he answered. "Leave him to shift for himself out here in the middle o' nowhere. So I can't do that to you either. C'mon now, squat, so's we c'n eat and get going again."

She was angry with him, but she did not permit her hurt feelings to make her do anything foolish like declining his offer of breakfast. They ate in silence. She avoided his eyes, looked away when he looked at her. When the coffeepot, the plates and the cups had been washed, dried and put away, and the fire had been smothered, and the idling mare had been saddled, Canavan's rifle was pushed down into the boot. He folded his blanket into a thick pad and laid it across Willie's back behind the saddle. He climbed up and at his insistence the girl handed him the box, and holding it in front of him he freed his left hand, and said as he reached down: "Lift your dress. You can't ride side-saddle 'less you wanna get bounced off."

When she raised her dress about even with the tops of her shoes, he frowned and said curtly: "Lift it higher. I've seen women's legs before, and I don't think yours c'n be any different from theirs. What's more, if you didn't show enough o' yourself when you were workin' in that Rogers' saloon, he'da fired you a long time ago instead o' keepin' you on."

He gave her no opportunity to answer. The moment she raised her dress high enough to permit her to straddle Willie, he caught her under her left arm and hoisted her onto the mare's back. She squirmed about in an effort to smooth out her dress under her, and finally settled herself comfortably.

"What d'you say? All set?" Canavan asked her.

"Yes!"

"Now comes the part you're really gonna love," he said, squaring around. "I don't wanna lose you. So you'd better put your arms around me and hang on."

She obeyed, curled her arms around his waist only to draw them back and get a firm grip on his pants belt. He made no comment, but simply nudged Willie with his knees, and the mare plodded away with them and shortly broke into a jog.

Three

There was no conversation between them. Apparently their silence must have puzzled the mare for she looked around at them several times rather wonderingly in the course of the long hours that followed. At about ten-thirty Canavan halted her in order to give her a breather and a chance to blow herself. While she stood a little spread-legged, Canavan helped the girl get down and then dismounted. He glanced at the girl. She stood with her back turned to him, looking back at the road over which they had come.

When the mare pawed the ground with her hoof, a sign that she was ready to go on again, Canavan patted her and climbed up on her. The girl came forward. Wordlessly he pointed to her box. She lifted it and he bent and took it from her. Again he settled it in front of him, and as before, reached down for her and with a slight heave of his left shoulder and a tightening of his left arm, swung her up behind him. He waited patiently for her to tell him when she was ready; when there was no word from her, he said over his shoulder: "Lemme know when you're all set."

"I'm all set now," she snapped.

"Thanks," he said dryly.

"You're welcome," she retorted.

Willie trotted away with them. Again neither Canavan nor the girl made any effort to talk. It was shortly after twelve when they made their second stop, this time for their midday meal. It consisted of generously heaped plates of hot cakes and coffee. They sat opposite each other and ate in silence. When Canavan was finished, he simply rose and stalked off. He was rinsing out the coffeepot when the girl brought him her plate and cup and sauntered away again. Ten minutes later they were again on the move.

At three o'clock they made their third stop. Again it was for the benefit of the mare, and only incidentally for them. Canavan stamped up and down and twisted his body from side to side as he sought to rid his thighs and back of the stiffness that had developed in them. He shot a look at his silent companion. She was standing in the middle of the road ranging her hand-shaded gaze over the open country southward.

"Y'oughta work your arms and legs a bit," he told her, "or you'll find yourself stiffened up."

She ignored him as though she hadn't heard him. He shrugged and held his tongue after that. He stood at Willie's head and patted her. In turn the mare whinnied softly and nuzzled him. After a while Canavan swung himself up into the saddle, and without looking around at the girl, said: "Let's go."

They were riding along about an hour or so later when the girl suddenly broke her silence. "Hope we don't have to spend another night sleeping out here."

Apparently the long ride had mellowed her. Canavan was tempted to say something about it, but decided against it. Instead he said: "Stage makes it to Hopewell in one day, doesn't it?"

"That's what I understood the driver to say."

"Then we will too."

"We aren't going very fast."

"I know. I've been holding Willie down because I didn't want to make it any tougher on you than I had to. You've been getting enough jouncing around."

She made no response to that. But after a brief silence, she asked: "What does 'JC' stand for?"

He knew where she had spotted his initials. They were pin-scratched in the metal heelplate of his gun.

"For my name," he replied. "For John Canavan."

"Oh," she said. "My name's Kowalski. Jenny Kowalski."

"Kowalski?" he repeated. "That's Polish, isn't it?"

"That's right. And Canavan—what's that, Irish?"

"Uh-huh."

"I thought you looked Irish. And that was even before I knew for sure."

"What'll you do if you don't find a job, or if you have to wait till one opens up for you?"

"Hopewell's a big town and there oughta be a lot o' saloons there. So there oughta be plenty o' jobs. And if there aren't and I don't hit it, I haven't gone hungry yet or without a place to sleep."

"Uh-huh," he said again.

They rode on in silence after that. It was evening when they sighted Hopewell, and just about seven o'clock when they wheeled into town and rode down what appeared to be the main street. Since it was the county seat it proved to be what Canavan expected, a good-sized town with fairly wide and intersecting streets. What surprised him though was the fact that save for the hotel which he spotted almost at once and a couple of rather widely separated stores whose

33

flickering lights were still burning against the gradually descending night, the rest of what he could see of the town was darkened and shuttered. What surprised him even more was the absence of glaring light and the usual sounds that he had come to associate with saloons. He made no mention of it, but chose instead to wait till Jenny noticed it.

She did shortly when she said: "Funny thing. But this is supposed to be a big, live town. But where are the saloons? Never heard o' them being anywhere else 'cept on the main street, and this looks to be it. Only I don't see a sign of even one."

"Maybe they have off nights," he suggested, "when they close at sundown."

"If they do, that's a new one on me. Far as I know, saloons never close."

"Well, don't go worrying about it just yet. Wait'll we get to the hotel. Then you can ask the clerk, or whoever else is around."

He reined in directly in front of the hotel, helped Jenny get down, then he dismounted. Carrying her box, he followed her into a cubicle of a dimly lit lobby. There was a spectacled, bald-headed man behind the counter that served as a desk, and another man who was leaning over it, talking with him.

When Jenny came up to the counter, the clerk nodded and said: "Evening, ma'am," while the other man straightened up and stepped back. Fairly tall and rather lean, he wore a star pinned to his shirtfront. He glanced mechanically at Canavan who had put down the box, then he looked at him a second time. He moved around Jenny and lifted his eyes to Canavan. "Think I know you," he said.

"Could be," Canavan answered, hitching up his gunbelt. "I've been places."

"So have I. Only we were both in the same place, say

34

ten, maybe even twelve years ago. It was down on the border. I don't remember your name, only that you were a Ranger and a heckuva man with your hands and your gun. I was a marshal then. My name's Hughes. Ben Hughes. Wanna take it from there?''

"Yeah, sure. We were both after the same man. Think his name was Harvey," Canavan offered with a grin.

"That's right."

"But being that you were a gover'ment man, you had first call on him. Think he was wanted for murder."

"Right again. He'd held up and robbed a mail car and killed the clerk in charge."

"We trailed him to a gambling joint and went in together after him and had to fight our way out've the place after we grabbed him and tried to take him out."

"Uh-huh," Hughes said, nodding. "Nothing the matter with your memory. Anyway, somebody threw a knife at me. I ducked but it caught me in the shoulder. You put a slug right smack in the middle of the knife thrower. A Mex he was. You half carried, half dragged me outta the place while I was still hangin' on to Harvey."

Canavan held out his big right hand; the local lawman grabbed it and pumped it vigorously.

"You're Irish and you've got an Irish name," he said. "And I've forgotten it and I'm ashamed o' myself."

"It's Canavan."

"Red Canavan," Hughes said instantly. "And I'm sure glad to see you again. If it hadn't been for you, I'da never made it outta there alive."

"Excuse me," Jenny said and both men looked at her. She addressed herself to Ben Hughes. "Canavan tells me all the saloons in town have closed. That right?"

Hughes nodded. "Town council decided we could get

35

along fine without the saloons and the women they had workin' in them. Being that the council hired me and pays me my wages, when they told me to close th'm up, I did just that. The saloonkeepers knew better'n to try and buck the law. So they loaded their stock and their women into their wagons and pulled out. Couple o' th'm headed west, the others went off in other directions.

"That's nice," Jenny said sarcastically. "So because some old pussyfooters with one foot in the grave objected to letting others enjoy themselves, they turned what I'd heard tell was a good, live town into a cemetery."

The sheriff smiled and said evenly: "We didn't shut down everything. We let a couple o' beer parlors stay open. If anybody wants booze instead o' beer and can't get along without it, there's no law that says he can't pull outta here and go somewhere's else. One thing I c'n tell you though, ma'am. Shuttin' down the saloons has made life for me and for our womenfolks a heckuva lot easier."

"I'm so glad," she said with a touch of anger in her voice.

She flashed him a hard, lip-curled look and turned her back on him. Canavan saw the bald-headed man hold out a key to her, and saw her snatch it out of his hand. The three men followed her with their eyes as she headed for a flight of uncovered stairs just beyond the lobby, and watched her go up.

When she topped the stairs and disappeared from view, Hughes said: "Can't please everybody, huh?"

"Waste o' time and effort to try," Canavan said.

When they heard a door on the upper floor open and then shut, Hughes remarked: "Kinda think the lady's mad."

36

"If she is she'll get over it."

"How long you gonna be around, Red?"

"Till tomorrow morning."

Hughes looked disappointed. "You hafta pull out that soon?"

"I'm heading for California," Canavan explained, "and that's a long ways off."

"I know."

"And being that I'm going, I wanna keep going and get there. Don't wanna make a career outta the trip."

"Will you stop by and have breakfast with me?"

"Yeah, sure, Ben."

"I'll look for you."

"Any place still open where I c'n get me some supper?"

"The Greek's. That's 'way down the street. Look, Red, you go put your horse away. I'll stop and tell Nick that you're a friend o' mine and to stay open awhile longer and that you'll be in say in what, half 'n hour or so?"

"That'll be fine."

The sheriff hitched up his pants belt, seemed to be debating something with himself, and finally asked: "Mind me asking your something, Red?"

"Mean you're wondering about the girl, and how she comes to be with me?"

"Yeah. But now that I think of it, it's none o' my business, and I shouldn't've asked. So forget it. See you tomorrow."

Canavan smiled. "It isn't anything like what you think, Ben. So there isn't any reason why I shouldn't tell you."

Without going into too much detail, Canavan told Hughes how Jenny and he had become acquainted. The sheriff listened attentively, and when Canavan finished, he simply said: "The stage company office is down the street too. Suppose I stop in there and tell Pete Horner who runs the line what happened and leave it to him to do what has to be done about the driver and the busted-down stage?"

"I'd be obliged to you, Ben."

"G'wan," Hughes retorted. "It's damned little I'm doing in return for what you did for me." He nudged Jenny's box with his boot toe. "This thing yours, Red?"

"No. Belongs to the girl. To Jenny."

Hughes turned to the bald-headed man and said: "Bick, be a good feller and tote this thing upstairs to the lady."

"Right, Sheriff," Bick responded. He looked at Canavan. "You want a room for tonight too, mister?"

"Yeah."

"I put the lady in number four. Number six is right next door. I'll hold that one for you."

"Thanks."

Canavan and Hughes left the hotel together. They stopped on the walk in front, briefly, for a last word before they parted for the night.

"Stable's up the street, Red."

They shook hands again. Then Hughes strode off down the street while Canavan crossed the walk to the curb, climbed up on Willie, wheeled her and headed up the street to the stable. Ten minutes later when he re-entered the hotel with his saddlebags draped over his shoulder and carrying his rifle, Bick handed him a key. Canavan trudged up the stairs, turned on the landing and stopped when he came to Jenny's room. There was a large white-lettered "4" on the door. He knocked and waited.

"Yeah?" he heard Jenny ask grumpily.

"It's me, Jenny. Canavan."

The floorboards creaked under her step. She opened the door. She was wearing the same kimono that she had worn the time she had burst in upon him. Turned-down lamplight somewhere behind her silhouetted her figure.

"Yeah?" she repeated.

"Hungry?"

"I suppose so."

"Gimme say five minutes to get cleaned up and we'll go get us something to eat."

"Mean there's a place still open in this graveyard?"

"Down the street. The man who runs it, a Greek named Nick, is waiting for us."

"I'll be ready when you are."

"Five minutes," he repeated.

She made no reply, simply stepped back and closed the door.

It was just about five minutes later when he returned for her, knocked again on her door and waited.

"It's open," she answered. "Come on in."

He opened the door and poked his head in. Jennie was standing in front of her bureau, peering into the looking glass at the top of it while she tried to hook up her dress at the back.

"Musta been outta my head when I let myself get talked into buying this thing," she muttered. "All o' my other dresses hook up the front. So I had to go and buy this one so's I'd have something else to aggravate me." He moved into the open doorway and halted there and watched her futile efforts to hook up her dress. She turned her head and looked at him and said crossly: "If you expect to eat tonight, you'd better come over here and see if you can hook me up."

As he advanced into the room he took off his hat,

dropped it in the chair that stood nearby, moved behind her and carefully hooked up the dress.

"All right?" she asked.

"Yep. All hooked up, and you look very nice in it."

"Thanks." Her box stood open against the opposite wall. She turned and took a jacket from it, turned again and held it out to him and said simply: "Please."

He took it from her, held it for her and helped her into it, turned and picked up his hat, clapped it on his head, walked to the open doorway, and half-turning, waited for her. She fussed briefly with her hair and came across the room. Standing in front of him she said: "Hope you've noticed that I didn't put on any o' what you called my warpaint. And no cologne either."

He smiled but made no comment. He pushed back against the doorjamb to permit her to pass, followed her out of the room and yanked the door shut. She handed him her key. He locked the door and returned the key to her and saw her put it in her jacket pocket. He followed her down the stairs. The lobby was deserted. They emerged from the hotel and marched down the street, Canavan's bootheels thumping rhythmically on the planked walk. The night was clear, the air crisp and clean-smelling.

"I had it all figured that this was gonna be the place for me," Canavan heard Jenny say, and he shot a look at her. "Wouldn'ta taken me any time at all to've gotten enough money together to pay the train fare, and there woulda been a little left over for a stake. Just my luck though that they took it into their fool heads to shut down the saloons. Y'know something, Canavan? That's the way it's been with me all my life. Every time I've made plans, something's always come up to spoil th'm for me."

"Y'know, there are a lot o'stores here in Hopewell,

and all kinds o' th'm too. Have you given a thought to getting yourself a job in one o' th'm?''

She stopped in her tracks. Fortunately Canavan was still looking at her. He jerked to a stop too.

"Aw, c'mon now," she said. "You oughta know better than that. Only kind o'work I've ever done has been in a saloon. Can you picture me working behind a counter selling something like ribbons or maybe yard goods?''

"How d'you know you wouldn't be able to make a go of it when you haven't tried?" he countered.

"I know what I can do and what I can't," she insisted.

"And I think you c'n do just about anything you set your mind to," he told her. "What d'you think o' that?''

"I don't think anything of it. You're trying to sweet-talk me into doing something that I know I'm not cut out for, and it's no go."

They walked on. A signboard that hung from a length of iron pipe that jutted out from the flat roof of a small building across the street and swung to and fro above the walk caught Canavan's eye. It bore a one-word legend: SHERIFF. Despite a curtain that spanned the lower half of the window and a shade that was drawn down to meet it but overlapped it and hung an inch or so below it, Canavan glimpsed turned-down lamplight in Hughes' office.

Jenny ranged her gaze after Canavan's, and said: "I don't think I like him."

"I do."

"Wanna know something, Mister Ranger? There were a couple o' times after you hauled me outta that stage when I didn't like you either. But you let me know right off that you didn't like my kind, so that made us

41

even. And what you did for me, you said you'd have done for anybody, even a dog. Case it means anything to you, although I don't think it does, I didn't feel flattered. No matter what you think o' me, I think I oughta rate a little higher than a dog."

"Of course you do, Jenny. A lot higher too. And I'm sorry I said that. That must be the place."

He took her by the arm and guided her across the walk to the Greek's place, stepped ahead of her, opened the door for her and followed her inside. It wasn't much of a restaurant, probably no more than a cut above a lunchroom. The absence of a counter and some stools constituted the only difference between them. A short, stocky, aproned man with a shock of iron-gray hair, metal-rimmed spectacles and a thick mustache with turned up ends appeared before them as Canavan closed the door.

That he was expecting Canavan was evidenced by the fact he simply pointed to a nearby table, one of some seven that crowded his establishment's floor space. "Sheriff say you don't have no sopper. So what you wanna eat? You like a nice steak maybe?"

Canavan laid his hat in the chair next to him. "Yeah," he said. "A steak'll be fine."

"For the lady too?"

"For the lady too," Canavan repeated. "And all the trimmings."

The Greek made no response. He simply trudged away to the rear. They sat in silence for a while, Jenny with her hands clasped and resting on the edge of the table and her eyes downcast. Suddenly she looked up at him and asked: "You got a wife somewhere?"

Canavan shook his head.

"But you did have one once, didn't you?"

42

"Uh-huh," he said, but he volunteered nothing beyond that.

"She walked out on you?"

"Nobody walked out on anybody."

"Then what happened to your wife?"

"She died in a fire."

"Oh, how awful!" Jenny exclaimed, and she shuddered. "Tell me about her."

"What d'you wanna know?"

"What was she like?"

"About your height, Jenny, brown hair and brown eyes."

"Pretty?"

"Very pretty."

"Go on."

"She was everything a man could ask for in a wife."

"Where were you when it happened?"

"I was away on an assignment at the time."

"Was it an accident?"

"No. She was visiting a cousin of hers. He'd refused to join in with some other cattlemen who wanted to drive some nesters out of the area. They got sore at him and late one night crept up to his house and set fire to it. When his wife, Beth, and he tried to break out, they were shot down."

"Was that your wife's name, Beth?"

"Yes."

"What happened to those cattlemen?"

"There were five o' th'm. I tracked th'm down, all of them, and I killed all five. That's why I had to quit the Rangers. For taking the law into my own hands."

She made no comment. Again she lowered her eyes and took to studying her hands.

"I suppose you'll be leaving here tomorrow," she

said after a brief silence.

"Right after breakfast."

"Think I oughta go back and ask Rogers to take me on again?"

"I'm afraid you'll have to decide that for yourself. You'd rather do that than try to find something to do here?"

"No, but I might have to. And that worries me. I'm afraid that if I go back, that'll be the end of California for me. And I want so to go there."

"Then don't go back."

She raised her eyes and seemed to be staring off into empty space beyond him.

"If I stay here and I do as you think I oughta, get me a job in one o' the stores even though I won't like it or be happy with it. . ."

"It's either that, like it or not, or Rogers. 'Course I know you won't get the kind o' money here that you were getting in a saloon and that it'll take you a lot longer to put away enough money to take you to California. Still—"

There was a sudden, startling roar of gunfire outside and Canavan sat upright. He started to get up from his chair when the stocky restaurant owner came running from the rear. He rushed past Canavan to the door, flung it open and stepped out on the walk, and looked up the street.

Twisting around, Canavan called to him: "What is it, Nick? Y'see anything?"

There was another burst of gunfire. Canavan pushed back from the table, leaped to his feet, whirled around and ran out. He skidded to a stop at Nick's side.

"The stage company," the latter told him, and pointed up the street.

"Y'mean it's a holdup?"

"Sure a holdup. There's the sheriff."

Canavan, shifting his gaze, saw Ben Hughes come bolting out of his office.

Hughes' gun was in his hand. He stopped momentarily at the curb and fired. Canavan couldn't see his target, only the answering flash of a gun somewhere up the street. Hughes staggered. A dark, shadowy figure lurhced across the walk some fifty feet up from where Canavan and Nick were standing, and suddenly pitched out from the curb and fell headlong in the gutter. Quickly Canavan shot a look in Hughes' direction. The sheriff was down on his hands and knees. As Canavan, loosening his own gun in his holster, dashed across the street to Hughes' side, the lawman sank down on his face and belly.

Four

Ben Hughes with his right arm outflung and his gun still gripped in his hand lay half in the gutter and half on the walk. Leaping over the curb, Canavan dropped to one knee at the sheriff's side. Just as he was about to bend over him movement diagonally across the street followed by the rush of booted feet attracted his attention, and he looked up instantly and saw first one shadowy figure and then a second one burst out of a darkened store and race up the street.

Canavan clawed for his gun and came up with it and fired twice. One of the running men, and by now the second one had overtaken his companion, stumbled, tripped over something, either a loose plank or his own feet, and fell. Canavan's third shot missed the first man who skidded on the walk and darted into an alley and disappeared. But in another moment there was a flurry of hoofbeats, and the man reappeared, not yet mounted but struggling to haul himself up into the saddle while his horse pranced about. He accomplished it finally, but only after he had kicked the skittish animal viciously, forcing him to stop his antics. The snorting horse carried him out to the gutter. As his rider wheeled him, Canavan fired again.

His bullet found its mark, causing the man to sag brokenly in the saddle. He toppled into the dirt. He fell heavily, landing on his shoulder and turned over on his belly. Propping himself up on his left elbow, he managed to draw his gun and level it. He pegged a shot at Canavan. But his aim was poor. Fired too high, the bullet struck and shattered a windowpane somewhere off to the left of Canavan. It fell in with a dust raising crash. Tinkling bits and slivers of glass spewed out over the walk.

Canavan replied. Again his bullet found his target. The fallen man slumped down on his face. One of his legs threshed convulsively, but only briefly. After a moment or so he lay still.

Canavan, who had been watching the man alertly with his gun, then became aware of lamplight flaming in windows on both sides of the street. Some of the windows were run up and heads were poked out. Most of the curious were men. In most instances they withdrew their heads shortly only to come hurrying out of their houses rifle or pistol-armed, some of them only half-dressed and several of them carrying lighted lanterns in addition to their weapons. As they poured into the street, other men came from other directions, and all converged upon the scene of the shooting.

A handful of them formed an uneven circle around the man who had stumbled and fallen on the walk, more of them gathered around the latter's companion who lay in the gutter. He was dragged over on his back and lantern light was played over him and shone in his face. Apparently he was a stranger for those who had a close look at him and failed to recognize him simply turned their backs on him and joined the other townsmen who were already standing around Hughes.

A lone man carrying a lighted lantern bent over the

holdup man who had exchanged shots with the sheriff only to fall with him. After a close look at him, the townsman came erect again and trudged across the street.

Lantern light revealed a small pool of blood under Hughes. Some of the blood had already run together with the dirt, puddling it. Carefully avoiding stepping in it, four men lifted Hughes and laid him on his back on the walk. Apparently someone living close by who had witnessed the shooting of the sheriff had lost no time in summoning the doctor, for now a coatless man carrying a small bag and followed by a limping townsman came hurrying up.

Those who were standing around Hughes moved apart so that the doctor could get to him. Bending over him and then kneeling at his side, the doctor motioned and lantern light was quickly played over the unconscious lawman. The doctor opened Hughes' shirt and his undershirt, baring his chest. Both shirts were bloodsoaked, his chest blood-smeared.

"Y'think he's dead, Doc?" someone asked.

The doctor was using his stethoscope on Hughes.

"If he's dead, it's a damned shame," someone else said. "A damned good man and one helluva good sheriff."

"Y'can say that again," a third man added. "And we're gonna have to look far an' wide to find another one like him."

"That's right," a man standing next to him said.

The doctor hung his stethoscope around his neck and got up. All eyes were on him.

"He's still alive," he announced, "so he's got a chance."

A murmur of relief swept through the crowd of on-lookers.

"But I can't do anything for him out here," the doctor continued. "Some of you carry him over to my office. But go easy with him. He's probably hemorrhaging now and careless handling of him may make things even worse."

Willing hands lifted the obviously well-liked Hughes, and with the doctor leading the way, the unconscious lawman was carried off around the corner. Those who stayed behind sent questioning glances at Canavan but he ignored them. Then a hand who had been standing on the fringe of the crowd sauntered over to Canavan, smiled and said: "You're a right handy man with your gun. Good thing you were around or those two holdup men would've got away."

Canavan look at him. The man was Bick.

"Oh," he said. "H'llo."

"I was standing in front o' the hotel gettin' a breath o' fresh air," Bick told him, "when those holdup men broke in on Pete Horner." Canavan's eyes followed Bick's when the latter looked across the street in the direction of the stage company's office. Now there was a light burning in it, and Canavan could see several men inside the place and others idling on the walk in front of it. "They musta gunned Pete down and grabbed up whatever cash they could lay their hands on, shot out the light and started to run for their horses. They'd left th'm in an alley a couple o' doors up from Horner's place. I saw the sheriff come outta his office on the run and shoot at one feller, a lookout I guess he was, who fired back at him. Then as he and Ben fell, I saw you come hustlin' across the street from the Greek's and take over for Ben. That was a nice thing for you to do, and a heckuva risky one too, and I thought the town council oughta know about it. So when I bumped into Al Lennart, he's the head man of the council, I buttonholed him and told him about you and what you'd done. I think the town owes you something.''

He smiled again and marched across the street. Canavan was following him with his eyes when there was a pluck at his sleeve. He turned his head. The girl was standing behind him.

"Jenny," he said. " 'Fraid I kinda forgot about you. Sorry.''

"You needn't be. You had more important things to 'tend to. You all right?''

"Yeah, sure.''

"How about the sheriff? He get hit bad?''

"Bad enough. Caught a slug in his chest.''

"Think he'll make it?''

"I sure hope so.''

"He's your friend. So I hope so too.''

He took her by the arm and led her to the corner to avoid having her pass too closely by the dead men and those who were standing around them. He could feel the onlookers' eyes following them and wondered if any of them had heard what Bick had said to him. Nick saw them coming, turned and hurried back inside.

As they stepped up on the walk, Jenny said: "People seein' you taking me by the arm will start talking once they know about me. Aren't you afraid o' what I'll do to your reputation?''

"Nope.''

As they reentered the restaurant Canavan drew his gun and reloaded it and holstered it again. He followed Jenny to the table that they had occupied earlier. Seating themselves, Canavan hunched over the table on his folded arms.

"We were talking about you goin' back to Rogers' place or stayin' on here," he began. He heard the street door open. When he saw Jenny raise her eyes and look past him, he asked: "S'matter?"

"A man," she replied low-voiced. "I think he's coming over here."

"All right. Let him come."

He did not turn his head when he heard approaching bootsteps and gave no sign at all when the man halted at their table. It was only when the latter said, "Excuse me," that Canavan lifted his gaze to him.

The man took off his hat, smiled at Jenny and said to Canavan: "My name's Lennart. I'm head o' the town council. Since you aren't eating yet, mind if I speak my piece and get done with it so's I don't interfere with what you're gonna eat when Nick gets to serving it?"

"Go ahead."

"You'll excuse me, ma'am?"

Jenny flashed him a smile. "Of course."

"Pull up a chair," Canavan suggested to him.

Lennart reached for the nearest chair, swung it around, and seated himself in it with his hat in his hands. He was about average in height but rather heavily built, his neatly combed hair gray in streaks through a healthy looking head of black.

"First off," he began, addressing himself to Canavan, "I think I ought tell you what I know about you. Your name's Canavan, you used to be a lawman, you're headed for California, and you and Ben Hughes are old friends." When Canavan nodded, Lennart continued. "Town owes you something for what you did tonight." He dug in his jacket pocket and produced a crinkly new fifty dollar bill and laid it on the table. "We'd like you to buy yourself something with this and call it a present from the people of Hopewell, a token of our appreciation. You'll be needing a couple o' pack horses on your trip west so the horses those three stickup men rode in on are yours. I've had them taken

51

down to the stable and they're keepin' your horse company."

"That's mighty generous of you," Canavan said. "But there wasn't any call for you to do anything in return for what I did tonight. Most of it was for Ben. The rest, guess having been a lawman for such a long time, when I see something happening, I just naturally have to take a hand in stoppin' it."

When Canavan sought to push the bill back to him, Lennart stopped him.

"No," he insisted. "That's yours."

"All right," Canavan said. "If that's the way you want it."

"It is."

"Thanks."

Lennart nodded. "Now think it'd be possible for you to lay over for a spell and carry on for Ben till he's up and around again and able to take over himself? We'd be only to glad to pay you same's we've been payin' him. 'Course we're gonna go on payin' him while he's laid up. We wouldn't think o' doing otherwise. Ben's done a top job for us and we appreciate it and him. What d'you think?"

"I'll wanna stay over for a while anyway," Canavan told him. "Because I'll wanna know how Ben's makin' out."

"Then it's a deal?" Lennart asked eagerly.

"Long's it doesn't mean that I have to lay over too long."

"I understand."

Lennart stood up, swung the chair around, and held out his hand. Canavan got up too and shook hands with him.

"Thank you, ma'am," Lennart said to Jenny.

He put on his hat and went striding out. As the door

closed behind him, Canavan picked up the bill, studied it, looked up at Jenny and said: "Well, what d'you know about that?"

"You deserve it. You earned it and more. You laid your life on the line for them and I'm glad they appreciate it." She smiled. "Y'know something? That's the first time anybody's ever trusted me the way he did, like I was somebody, like I was a lady. And I kinda liked it. 'Course," she added quickly, "I realize he treated me with such respect because of you. Even so—"

She stopped when Canavan folded the bill in two and pushed it across the table into her hands. She stared at it and flushed and finally lifted wide eyes to him. "What's that for?"

"I think that oughta cover your train fare to California and leave you enough to keep you eating for a while after you get there. So forget about Rogers and everything else and dig into your steak when it gets here and enjoy it."

She was still staring at him a moment later when Nick brought them their steaks.

"Ah," Canavan said after he had cut into his and had chewed a small piece. "That's good." When there was no response from Jenny, he looked up. She hadn't touched her steak. She sat headbowed. When he saw a tear trickle down her cheek, he put down his knife and fork. "Hey, what is it? What's the matter? What are you cryin' for?"

She didn't answer. He leaned over the table, put a big finger under her chin and raised her head. There were more tears in her eyes.

"You're the first man, in fact the first anybody who's ever given me anything," she told him. "I owe you so much already without this, and you keep givin' me more."

"You don't owe me a thing. Here," he said, and he produced a clean, neatly folded bandana and held it out to her. She took it. Without unfolding it, she dabbed at her eyes with it, dried her tears and handed it back to him. As he pocketed it, he said: "Now go to work on that steak. Don't let it get cold."

She obeyed, began to ply her knife, but stopped shortly and meeting his eyes, "It isn't right. You aren't responsible for me or for what happens to me," she said.

"Eat," he commanded.

"You aren't that flush that you c'n hand over a fifty just like that."

"No, I'm not flush. But I'm not hurting for anything either, and that includes cash. G'wan now. Eat."

She didn't answer, simply proceeded to eat as he had directed. But she ate in silence.

Nick came to their table and said: "Got it nice opple pie. You like some?"

"Yes," Canavan told him. "And coffee."

"For the lady too?"

"For the lady too," Canavan repeated gravely.

Nick looked at Jenny. "Steak is good, lady?"

"Very good," she answered.

Obviously satisfied, Nick turned and plodded away. He returned shortly with their coffee and two generous cuts of pie, and again left them alone.

Half an hour later when they left the Greek's and started up the street Canavan was quick to note that the bodies of the dead men had been removed and that the lamps that had been lighted after the attempted holdup were still burning, holding off the darkness. There were little knots of men still standing about here and there, a sign that the excitement that had awakened them and brought them out to the street had aroused them to such a pitch that they had no desire to go back to bed. Appraising eyes were lifted to Jenny and Canavan as they marched along.

As they neared a group that was standing on the walk in front of the stage company's office, Al Lennart, detaching himself from the others, stepped forward, lifted his hat to Jenny and said to Canavan: "Hate to have to tell you this, Canavan. But Ben Hughes is dead. Never came to and died on Doc Morris' table. Knowing the Doc the way I do, I c'n tell you he musta done everything he could to save Ben. But it was no go. I'm sorry."

"So am I."

"We'll be burying Ben and Pete Horner tomorrow morning say around nine. Horner was the feller who ran the stage line office here."

"I know. Hughes told me about him."

"He had less a chance than Ben did. When those three skunks busted in on him, they blasted him to bits," Lennart continued. Then he added in a lighter tone: "Meantime I'll be getting in touch with a couple o' good men I've heard of who might be able to handle Ben's job. Soon's I hear anything worthwhile, I'll let you know so's you'll be able to figure on when you c'n head out."

"Right."

"You c'n move into Ben's place any time you like. I think you'll find he kept it nice an' clean. That's the kind o' man he was."

"Think I'd rather stay put in the hotel."

Lennart shrugged. "Up to you."

Canavan and Jenny walked on.

"I'm sorry about that man Hughes," Jenny said shortly.

"They're gonna have t'do a lot o' lookin' around

before they come up with another man like him."

Bick was behind the counter working on a long column of scribbled figures on a page in a worn ledger, a stub of a pencil gripped between his teeth, when they entered the hotel. He looked up when he heard their step. He took the pencil out of his mouth. "You hear about the sheriff?" he asked.

Canavan nodded. "Lennart just told me. Oh, and thanks for giving me such a buildup to him."

Bick smiled and returned to his figures as they headed for the stairs. He looked up again as they made their way up, followed them briefly with his eyes, and began to add the figures as they topped the stairs and turned on the landing. They halted when they came to Jenny's room.

"Shoulda asked Bick about the trains," Canavan said. "No point in you hangin' around here any longer'n necessary being that you're all set to go."

"I didn't know you were in such a sweat to get rid o' me," Jenny said with a little smile parting her lips.

"I'm not."

"Aw, c'mon now! If I let myself believe that, the next thing you'll pull on me will be how much you know you're gonna miss me when I'm gone."

He shrugged wordlessly.

"I wish you liked me. Even a little. Instead o' just putting up with me."

"How d'you know I don't like you?" he demanded. She was taken back by his sharp tone. "You don't know it but I didn't like the idea of you even thinkin' of goin' back to work for Rogers. No more'n I did of leavin' you here and knowing how unhappy you'd be doing something you had no liking for. I'd already made up my mind to stake you to a ticket and something extra to keep you going once you got out to California. 'Course having Lennart come through with that fifty dollars made it easy for me. So y'see you don't know all the answers. Must be the kind you've gotten used to dealing with in those lousy saloons has got you thinking that everybody's the same. You couldn't be more wrong.''

She moved closer to him. Her hands came up and gripped his arms. Suddenly she was pressing herself against him with her arms climbing upward and curling themselves around his neck. She brought his head down and kissed him hard on the mouth. The pressure of her supple young body against his and her kiss rekindled something deep down inside of him. His arms came up to encircle her and crush her to him. But something stopped him and he drew his arms down.

"That was nice," he said. "But what was it for?"

"Does there have t'be a reason for everything? Maybe I just felt like doing it. Or maybe it was my way o' saying thanks."

He didn't say anything. She bowed her head against his chest and whispered: "Something's happened to me, John. All of a sudden I find I've lost my nerve. And it's because o' you." He held her off at arms' length and peered into her face, plainly puzzled by what she had said. "I've come to look to you to do whatever's to be done. And without you to turn to, once I get on that train, I'm gonna feel lost. Sure I want to get out to California. But I'm afraid I'm not going to feel up to takin' on a lot o' strangers. Up until you came along, nothing ever fazed me. Now I've got a kind o' sinking feeling deep down inside o' me. Let me go out there with you, John. Please."

"But I'm tied down here. You know that. Leastways, till Lennart finds himself a new man for the sheriff's job."

"I know, and I don't care. I can wait till you're ready

to go. And I'll promise you this. I won't do anything to embarrass you or make you ashamed o' me. I handled myself like a lady tonight, didn't I, in front o' that Lennart? Well, that's the way I intend to—''

She stopped when they heard a voice downstairs that both of them recognized as Lennart's.

"No, you don't have to call him, Bick. Just tell me what room he's in and I'll go up myself. Got something important to talk to him about.''

"It's No. 6, Al,'' they heard Bick say.

"We'll go into this later,'' Canavan told Jenny, and they parted, she going into her room and he into his.

He had just struck a light in the lamp when he heard Lennart's step outside his room, then his knock on the door. Canavan delayed answering it for a moment or two, then he strode to the door and opened it.

"Hello again,'' the heavily built councilman said with a wry grin. "Got something to discuss with you if you've got a minute and a mind to listen.''

"I've got both,'' Canavan replied and backed with the door and closed it again after his visitor.

The latter stepped inside, took off his hat and put it on the bureau.

"I've been talking with the other members of the council,'' he began, "and they think that instead o' us lookin' around for somebody else to pin Hughes' star on that we might be missing a good bet by not makin' you a real good offer to get you to forget about California and stay put here. You wanna hear more, or is it California and nothing else but?''

"'Fraid that's what it is.''

Lennart looked disappointed.

"Well,'' he said, "if that's the way it is with you, then I don't suppose there's any point in goin' on with things. 'Less of course you wanna sleep on it and let me

58

know for sure tomorrow morning before I go gettin' in touch with some others who might be interested in the job. Y'know, things have a way of looking different after you've had a chance to sleep on th'm. We're willing to sweeten the pay to sixty-five bucks a month to keep you here. That's the story."

Canavan smiled. "I've worked for a heckuva lot less."

"Uh-huh. That's why I figured this might be something you wouldn't wanna pass up."

Lennart took his hat from the bureau and put it on, nodded to Canavan, turned and walked to the door. "G'night."

"G'night," Canavan responded.

He followed Lennart to the door and closed it after him. He stood motionlessly for a time, listening to the councilman's fading footsteps. When he was satisfied that Lennart had gone, he left his room and tapped lightly with his fingertips on Jenny's door. There was no answer. Instead the door was opened very quietly. As he stepped inside he noticed that the light in the lamp that stood where his did, on the bureau, had been turned down to its very lowest. He noticed too that the window shade had been drawn to the sill. Jenny closed the door and stood backed against it. As he turned to her, she said: "I was standing behind the door and listening."

"He wanted to know if I'd be willing to forget about California and stay on if they raised the ante," he told her.

"Oh?"

"I turned him down. But because he asked me to I agreed to sleep on it and let him know tomorrow. But my answer won't be any different then."

"I hope you aren't turning him down because o' me."

"I don't want the job. I quit bein' a lawman a long time ago, and I wanna stay quit." When she made no comment, he continued. "I'll give him a reasonable length o' time to get himself a new sheriff. Say a week or so. But if he hasn't tied on to somebody by that time, that'll be it. We'll go on our way."

"Whenever you say the word, I'll be ready to go. Oh, unhook me, will you please?"

She turned herself around. He unhooked her dress and stepped back from her and she turned to him again.

"I tried unhooking it myself. But I couldn't make it."

"Ever drive a wagon?" he asked her.

"A wagon?" she repeated. "Yeah, sure. But that was a long time ago. When I was a kid. But why d'you ask? We gonna go by wagon?"

"If I c'n make a deal for one with the stableman. Oughta be a lot more comfortable living and sleeping in a wagon."

"And how it oughta. I don't think much of sleeping out in the open."

"And it'll be a lot better if we run into rain."

"That's right. Hey, you think of everything, don't you?"

"Let's say I try to. Well, time to turn in. It's been a long day for both of us. I'm kinda beat and you must be too. Oh, don't forget to lock your door."

Half-turning she took the key out of the door and handed it to him. He looked at her wonderingly.

"You lock it," she said. "From the outside. Case I'm still asleep when you're ready for breakfast, and chances are I'll still be pounding my ear by then bein' that I'm not used to gettin' up early, come in and wake me. You mind?"

"No, 'course not."

"All right with you if I call you Johnny? John sounds kinda stiff to me."

He smiled. "Johnny'll be fine."

"G'night," she said and offered him her lips.

He kissed her lightly. "G'night, Jenny."

"Thanks for everything."

"Forget it."

"Johnny. . ."

"Yeah?" he asked with his hand on the doorknob.

"If we don't hit it off right, it won't be because I won't have tried. Fact is, I aim to try harder to please you than I've ever tried doing anything before."

"I'm sure we'll get along just fine. So don't worry about it."

She moved back from the door. He opened it and went out and drew it shut. When she heard the key grate and turn in the lock, she sauntered away from the door, taking off her dress at the same time.

Five

Canavan awoke at dawn the next morning. Turning on his side and leaning out of his bed, he raised a corner of the threadbare window shade and peered out. The thinning night shadows had already begun to lift and dissolve, revealing the street in all its shabbiness. It was hushed and deserted, its shops still shuttered and locked up tight. A gust of wind that came sweeping into town from the open prairie flung dust and dead, curled up leaves over the narrow walk opposite the hotel, and then changing direction veered away to about the middle of the gutter, half-turned a second time and raced up the street and fled out of town. The sky, Canavan noticed, when he raised his gaze briefly, was empty and grayish. He let go of the shade and it dropped back in place over the window, shutting out the dawn light. However some thin rays of light sifted into the room through the cracks in the shade.

It was far too early, he knew, for Jenny to be awake or for him to wake her. So he slumped down again on his back and stared up at the ceiling. He spied a cobweb in a far corner of the room where the right-angling walls and the ceiling came together. But he forgot about it when he suddenly thought he heard sounds of movement in Jenny's room. He kicked off the covers, swung his long legs over the side of the bed and stood up on his bare feet and winced because the uncovered floor was cold. He pressed his ear to the wall between the two rooms and listened. But he couldn't hear anything. After a minute or so, deciding that he must have imagined it, he returned to his bed, drew up the covers and lay back again.

His thoughts went back to the previous night, particularly to Jenny rather than to any of the other happenings. He had been thinking about her when sleep had overtaken him. Now that he was fully awake, he began to wonder if he had let himself in for trouble by letting her persuade him to take her along with him. Yet how could he have avoided agreeing to it? He couldn't have refused her without being cruel, and even though she wasn't the kind of woman to whom he would have been attracted under ordinary circumstances, he had no desire to hurt her. Despite her saloon-acquired worldliness, once the hard crust had been stripped away, she was just an average woman with an average woman's weaknesses and an unconcealed desired for a strong man to serve as a buffer between her and the world.

Something that she had said came back to him and bothered him. While he wasn't certain of her exact words, as he recalled it, it was something to the effect that she would try harder to please him than anything she had ever tried doing before. No woman would ever say anything like that, he told himself, unless she had something in mind, and quite obviously what Jenny had in mind had to do with marriage. Then he recalled something else that she had said. That was just before he had left her. If they didn't hit it off right, it wouldn't be because she hadn't tried. Both things confirmed his fears. She was going to do her best to make herself the kind of woman he would want for his wife.

"Well, if that's it, and it figures it must be, then it sure looks to me like I've let myself in for a helluva lot more'n I bargained for when I hauled her outta that busted down stage," he thought to himself. "Now the only trouble is that I don't know of any way o' backin' outta the deal without hurting her. All I'd have to do is up an' tell her that I've changed my mind about takin' her with me. That'd be one helluva slap in the face for her. Just goes to show you how a man c'n get himself in something way over his head by tryin' to do somebody a good turn."

Again he kicked off the covers and, making a wry face in anticipation of stepping onto the cold floor, made a lunge for his clothes and brought them back to the bed with him, and sitting in the very middle of it, proceeded to get into them. He filled the basin with water from the pitcher and poked a big finger into it. It was cold, and the thought of washing and shaving with it was anything but appealing. For a moment he considered tramping downstairs and getting Bick to rustle up some hot water for him. But sensing that it was too early for Bick to be up and about, he abandoned the idea.

Some fifteen minutes later, still chilled by the cold water, he locked the door to his room and moved on to Jenny's. He put his ear to the door. But there was no sound of any kind from within her room. He tapped lightly a couple of times on the door. When there was no response, he frowned, inserted the key in the lock and turned it and opened the door the barest bit, and peered in. She lay huddled up, with the covers drawn up so high about her that only the very top of her head was visible.

"Jenny," he whispered.

She didn't answer. She didn't move either. He glided inside on tiptoe, debating with himself whether to touch her and wake her as she had instructed him to, or to let her sleep.

"Come right down to it," he thought to himself, "there isn't any reason for her to get up this early just because I'm up."

Noiselessly he backed out, closing the door quietly and returned to his own room. In one of the bureau drawers he found a piece of paper and in still another drawer a stub of a pencil and proceeded to write her a note.

I'll be over at the office. When you're ready to eat, come over.

Once again he tiptoed into her room and ranged his eyes around it, looking for a good place to leave the note. When he failed to find the kind of place that suited his purpose, he backed out again, locked the door from the outside, got down on his knees and laying the key on top of the note, managed to slip both things under the door. Then he turned and went down the stairs. The tiny lobby was deserted, the desk, behind which he had gotten used to seeing Bick posted, unmanned.

"Must be poundin' his ear same's Jenny is," he muttered to himself as he passed it and strode out.

Halting on the walk in front of the hotel, he sent his gaze over the street. It was still hushed and deserted. He lifted his eyes. There was a tiny, flickering glimmer of candlelight in the dawn sky. But as he watched, it began to spread. It grew stronger and burned steadily and soon the entire sky was filled with brightening light, a sign that it was day. A brisk wind came spinning into town. But it was empty-handed and left nothing behind it as it flashed up the street.

When Canavan heard slow, almost measured,

scuffing bootsteps, he looked in their direction. The slope-shouldered figure of the unhappy lunchroom owner came into view and Canavan held his gaze on him as he came steadily closer, and watched him unlock his door and step inside. Moments later Canavan saw the night light at the rear of the place go out. He sauntered across the street and entered the lunchroom.

The owner poked his head out of the kitchen. "You're the feller who doesn't like to sleep," he grunted.

"Only when I'm hungry," Canavan responded, straddling a stool, thumbing his hat up from his forehead and hunching over the lip of the counter on his folded arms.

"What d'you wanna eat?"

"Oh, some coffee and a couple o' buns oughta do me for now."

"Gimme ten minutes."

"You've got th'm," Canavan said.

He sat motionlessly for half a minute or so, then hoisting himself up from the stool, hitched up his pants and sauntered over to the open doorway. Halting astride the worn metal threshold strip, he stood there, gazing about him. Now there were signs of activity and proof that the town had finally awakened. A couple of aproned storekeepers who had already unlocked their doors and removed the shutters from their windows were sweeping off the dust and leaf-strewn walk that fronted their establishments. Canavan heard a window run up somewhere up the street. Then from the opposite direction came the shrill voice of a woman. A dog barked and a man ordered the dog to be quiet. The dog obeyed. There was a brief silence. Then Canavan heard the woman's voice a second time. The man yelled something back at her, and this time the woman held her tongue. Canavan grinned fleetingly. A man came striding down the opposite side of the street. Canavan leveled a long look at him and recognized him as he came closer. It was Al Lennart. Canavan stepped out on the walk and waited. When Lennart neared the hotel and glanced across the street and saw Canavan idling in front of the lunchroom, he angled over, stepped up on the walk, and gave Canavan a nod. "Morning."

"Morning," Canavan responded.

"I was gonna leave this for you with Bick," the councilman said. "But when I saw you standing here. . ." He didn't finish but fished in his pants pocket and finally produced a key that he handed to Canavan. "That's your office key. You'll find Hughes' star layin' on the desk. Put it on like a good feller so folks around will know that the law's on the job and that you're it."

"Right," Canavan said, and put the key in his shirt pocket.

"What'd you decide?"

"Sorry to disappoint you, but it's still California for me soon's you come up with somebody to take over the job."

"I was afraid that that'd be your answer," Lennart said, managing a wry smile. "But I kept hoping anyway that you'd take us up on our offer and stay put. And while I'm disappointed, I can't rightly say I blame you. California's new and big, and judging by what I've heard tell, it's rich country too. So you oughta do all right there for yourself."

"I sure hope so."

"Soon's the funeral's over, I'll get busy sending out some letters. While I don't expect to come up with anybody as good as you or Ben Hughes, long as one o' th'm looks like he might be able to do a passable job for us, we'll have to settle for him." When there was no comment from Canavan, Lennart said: "See you in church."

"Yeah, sure. You mind telling me where it is?"

"'Round the corner from the Greek's. Funeral's set for nine o'clock. Try to make it a mite earlier than that so's things can get started on time. Reverend Mayberry doesn't like to be kept waiting."

Lennart marched off and Canavan slowly returned to the lunchroom doorway. After a few minutes, just when he was about to retrace his steps to his stool, the grinding spin of wagon wheels and the measured thump of horses' hoofs made him look up the street. A stagecoach came rumbling into town. Behind it came a second one. Both pulled up at the curb in front of a shop whose window bore the word BARBER in large letters. There was something else below that in much smaller letters that Canavan had to crane his neck and look hard at it before he was able to make out the words "Undertaker."

An aproned man emerged from the shop and talked briefly with the drivers of the two stages who had already climbed down from their perches. Then the three converged upon the second stage. The door to it was opened and held back. Canavan saw a canvas-wrapped body lifted out. It was the body, he told himself, of the driver of Jenny's stage. The three men carried the dead man into the shop. As the door to it closed behind them, Canavan returned to his stool. He was washing down the last of three buns with a second cup of coffee when he heard a light step. He glanced in the direction of the open door. The newcomer was Jenny.

"Good morning," he said, getting to his feet. "I was just having a little something to hold me till you were ready for breakfast."

"I'm ready now."

He gulped down the rest of the coffee. "Mind if we eat here?"

"No, 'course not."

He helped her seat herself on the stool next to his, took off his hat and put it on still another stool.

"Why didn't you wake me?" she asked Canavan.

"It was so early and you were fast asleep, so I figured I'd give you say an hour more, then if you didn't get up, I'd go back upstairs and wake you."

"I look all right?"

He drew back a little and looked at her. "You look fine," he told her.

"Even without my warpaint?"

He grinned at her. "Even better without," he replied.

"I chucked it together with that cologne you didn't like."

"Oh?"

"I wanna get rid of just about everything I've got with me," she continued, "and get me a couple o' plain little dresses that hook up the front and that can stand hard wear. And a pair o' plain shoes."

He nodded. "Get 'em outta that fifty."

"Nope," she said with a shake of her head. "I've got enough o' my own dough to get me what I need and to keep me going till we pull outta here." She smiled and added: "Then I'll be living offa you."

"You'll earn your keep."

"I aim to," she said gravely. "One of the first things you're gonna do once we get going is teach me how to cook. That's a woman's job and I aim to do that along with whatever else there will be for me to do. Oh, before I forget this," and she put her hand in her jacket pocket, produced the fifty dollar bill and handed it to him. "I won't need it."

He shrugged. "All right," he said and pocketed the bill. "But if you run short I want you to tell me so I c'n give you some. Understand?"

"Haven't anyone else to turn to, or anyone else I'd want to turn to. So if I need 'nything, I'll let you know quick."

"That's what I want you to do."

"What time's the funeral?" Jenny asked.

"Nine. Don't think it's eight yet. So we've got plenty o' time."

The angular lunchroom owner came out of the kitchen., "What c'n I fix for you, lady," he asked Jenny.

"I'd like a fried egg, please, and some coffee."

"And you, mister?"

"I'll have the same," Canavan answered.

Half an hour later they left the lunchroom. As they neared the sheriff's office, Canavan said: "Have to stop at the office for a minute. Lennart wants me to wear Ben's star."

Jenny waited outside while Canavan unlocked the door and went in. Minutes later with Hughes' star pinned to the flap of his shirtpocket, he opened the door intending to call Jenny and have her come inside so that she might see how neat and orderly Hughes had maintained the office and his living quarters.

He stopped abruptly in the half-opened doorway and watched a beefy man attired in city-tailored clothes and carrying a small cloth-covered valise come rushing across the street with a glad cry of "Hey, Jenny!" and throw both arms around her. She struggled to free herself. But the man laughed and held her tight, saying, "You used t'be glad to see me whenever I hit Rogers' place."

"Let go o' me, you—you fat slob!" Canavan heard

her rage at the man who looked like a drummer.

Canavan poked him in the back with a big finger.

"Let go of her," he said evenly.

"It's all right, partner. She's an old girlfriend o' mine. And in her own way I know she's glad to see me."

Jenny kicked him in the shin and he released her for a moment. "Hey, what's the idea? That hurt!" he said and reached for her a second time.

Canavan curled a muscular arm around the man's neck and tightening his arm, dragged him away, and with a mighty heave sent him careening across the walk. Stumbling and tripping over his own feet, he fell in the gutter on his backside and stared wide-eyed into Canavan's face when the latter bent down in front of him.

"There's a stage up the street," Canavan told him. "Go ask the driver when he's due to pull out so's you c'n be on it."

"What's idea?" the man, suddenly red-faced, sputtered. "I didn't do anything."

"I know. But just to make sure you don't do it again, be on that stage when it heads out."

"But I've got business here," the man protested. "What's more I've got friends here. So you can't run me out just like that."

Canavan pointed to his star. "Wanna bet?"

"Oh, the law, huh?" the man said. "All right, Sheriff. I'll go find out about that stage right away."

"Now that's what I call using your head," Canavan said. He gave the man a hand and hauled him to his feet. "Better dust off the seat o' your pants. You've got some o' the gutter sticking to it."

He watched the man hurry across the street in the direction of the idling stages and saw him slap himself on the backside with his right hand in an effort to rid himself of the dirt that his encounter with the gutter had attached to him. As he neared the first stage Canavan saw one of the drivers come out of the barber shop. The drummer and the driver stopped to talk.

Turning and stepping up on the walk, Canavan said to Jenny: "There's a looking glass on the wall in the office. You can straighten your hat in there."

He moved past her to the half-opened door, held it wide and followed her inside and mutely pointed to the looking glass. Standing tight-lipped and a little flushed in front of it, she straightened her hat and smoothed down her dress. "I'm sorry for what happened. I didn't mean to make a scene."

"It wasn't your fault," Canavan said.

"I know. But I'm still sorry it happened. Those people who were watching from across the street, I can imagine what they must have been thinking."

"They can think anything they like long's I don't hear them say anything. Let's go."

He followed her outside. Again she waited on the walk, this time while he locked the door. He had ignored the townspeople who had been standing across the way before. Now he stopped and looked hard at them. Apparently they understood the look he gave them for they moved so suddenly and so awkwardly that they collided with one another. It was plain that many of them had heard of his exploits the previous night. And this time all of them had seen him manhandle the hapless drummer. They had no desire to have him manhandle them.

As they scurried away, Canavan took Jenny by the arm and led her to the corner, crossed the street with her and passed the Greek's place. Rounding the next corner they slowed their step when they saw a number of people crowding the walk in front of a building that

Canavan took to be the church. Closer at hand though was a small group of men who were talking quietly among themselves. Lennart was one of the group.

As Canavan and Jenny neared them, Lennart lifted his hat to Jenny and smiled. "Morning, Ma'am."

Jenny responded with a smile and a murmured "Good morning."

A couple of the other men touched their hats to her too. Most of those who were idling directly in front of the church were bonnetted women. Some of them eyed Jenny critically and she stared back at them stonily. Others smiled at her politely as Canavan led her past them and into the church. They seated themselves in the last row. The church was about half-filled, Canavan noticed, as he sat on the hard bench. There was a general turning of heads, most of them women's, and Canavan, glancing at Jenny out of a corner of his eye, saw her flush.

"Take it easy," he told her in a low voice. "Don't let them get you."

"Old biddies," he heard her say. "Word gets around fast, doesn't it? By the time we get outta here every woman will hear what happened and soon's they get home their neighbors'll hear about it and the first thing I know even the kids will be giving me dirty looks."

Both turned and looked when there were heavy boot-steps behind them. Four men carrying a plain wooden coffin filed down the aisle and placed it upon two wooden horses. They trudged out but returned shortly with a second coffin, and this one too was lowered onto a pair of horses. The people who had been waiting outside trooped in and soon the church filled up. The minister, a thin, pinch-faced individual, appeared and the service began. It was surprisingly brief.

When the service was over and the coffins were

carried out, Canavan nudged Jenny. "Let's go."

She rose without a word when he did. Together they walked out. An open wagon that had its body, wheels and shafts painted black held the coffin. Canavan glanced at Jenny a couple of times as they neared the corner and rounded it. She was tight-mouthed and silent. They passed the Greek's and turned up the street. Still she held her tongue.

As they came directly opposite his newly acquired office, she finally said: "You've got a job to do. So you'd better go do it. I'm going back to the hotel."

"And do what there, just sit and then sit some more, and let those gossipy women force you to hide? What about having something to eat later on?"

"I'll let you know then. Right now the thought of eating anything sickens me."

He made no attempt to leave her, and if she was aware of it, she didn't say anything. When they entered the hotel, the tiny lobby and the counter were deserted. Jenny leaned over the counter and studied the board on the back wall that held the room keys. Canavan pointed wordlessly to a white-painted "4" on the board and Jenny lifted the key off the nail above the numeral. He followed her up the stairs and turned after her on the shadowy landing and waited patiently while she unlocked her door and trooped inside at her heels. He closed the door and backed against it. She took off her hat and put it on the bureau, removed her jacket and tossed it on the box that held her clothes, perched herself on the edge of the box and finally looked up at him.

"It's no good, Johnny," she said. "It's no good and it won't work. So I'm not going with you." When he made no answer, she went on. "Everywhere we go, there'll always be a chance o' me running into somebody who used to come into Rogers' place and who'll remember me from there. It'll be embarrassing for you and there's liable to be trouble, and you're the last one I'd ever want to hurt. You've been too good to me for that. You've treated me like I was, well, a somebody, and while I've liked that and even enjoyed it, somebody could pop up most anywhere and we'd have what happened today all over again. And I don't want that. If I'm alone and it happens, that's one thing. But when it happens when I'm with you, I feel ashamed, even dirty because you're decent and clean and I'm fresh out've a saloon. So if you'll find out for me if there's a stage outta here tonight headed east—"

"Nope," Canavan said curtly. "I'm not gonna do anything o' the kind because you aren't going anywhere except west and with me when I'm ready to go. Now get this straight, Jenny. If anybody has the right to back out, it's me. Not you. I didn't invite you to come along with me. You invited yourself. It was all right with me then and it's still all right with me now. So I don't wanna hear 'nymore outta you about you changing your mind and quitting on me."

"I was only thinking of you, Johnny," she answered, averting her eyes. "I wanted to save you from the embarrassment that's sure to come every time somebody reco'nizes me and from the way people look at me once they know I used to work in a saloon."

"I think I'm man enough to handle anyone and anything that c'n come up," he retorted. "So don't you go worrying about me."

"All right," she said.

In a gentler tone than he had used before, he said: "You said you need a couple o' dresses and shoes, and maybe you'll think o' some other good things you want too once you're in the store. You're gonna get th'm now, and anybody who even looks sideways at you is gonna wish he hadn't because I'm gonna trail along with you and they'll get it good from me. It's warm out. So you won't need your hat or your jacket. Soon's we get you fixed up, I'll go get started earning my wages. C'mon.''

He stepped back from the door, opened it and held it wide, turned his head and looked at her.

"Well?" he asked her. "Time's a-wasting, y'know."

She got up slowly. Slowly too she came across the room to him. There were tears in her eyes. He frowned, took out his bandana and held it out to her. She took it, dried her tears and returned the bandana to him.

He removed the key and followed her out, closed and locked the door, and put the key in his pocket. Together they went down the landing, trooped downstairs, and passed through the deserted lobby out to the street.

"Which way?" he wanted to know.

"Up the street, I think."

Side by side, they walked up the street. When they came to a double-windowed store, they stopped, and Jenny peered in through the open door, turned and nodded to him, and led the way inside. There was a wooden rack of dresses opposite the door. Jenny headed for it and began to look through the dresses while Canavan drifted away from the door and leaned against the counter.

A man, average-sized and rather thin-faced, obviously the proprietor, came from the rear, looked at Jenny, frowned and said coldly: "I don't think any o' those will suit you. Why don't you try one o' the places across the way like Schwab's? The women from the saloons uster go there because Mrs. Schwab uster stock the low cut, frilly things they went for."

"Mean you'd rather not sell me?" Jenny asked.

"That's the general idea," the storekeeper answered bluntly.

"If you see anything you like, take it, Jenny," Canavan said, and the storekeeper who hadn't noticed him standing quietly off to a side jerked his head around and crimson-faced, stared at him with wide, fearful eyes.

"If our righteous friend objects, I'll shove the rack down his throat and make him eat it."

The man gulped and swallowed hard. "Don't get me wrong, mister," he said, swallowing again. "'Course I don't object to the little lady's lookin' at what I've got and pickin' out whatever strikes her fancy. Heck, that's what I'm in business for."

"Hmm," Canavan said.

Jenny selected three dresses, and turning to Canavan, held each one up in front of her so that he might see them. Each time he nodded and each time Jenny laid the approved selection across the storekeeper's arm.

The latter laughed a little hollowly. "Gotta hand it to the little lady, mister. She sure knows what's nice." Then he turned to Jenny. "Anything else you want? Maybe you'd like to take a look around?"

"I need a pair of shoes," Jenny answered. "Oh, and a couple of petticoats."

"Yes, ma'am. You mind coming this way?"

Fifteen minutes later, with the dresses draped over Jenny's arm and Canavan carrying a paper-wrapped package that contained her other purchases, they turned to go. The storekeeper followed them to the door.

"Been a pleasure waitin' on you, little lady," he said. "If there's anything else you need, I sure hope you'll come in and let me show you what I've got. I keep a pretty full stock, you know."

As they came to the open doorway to the hotel,

Canavan slowed his step a little and grinned. "After you, little lady."

Jennie stopped, turned, and gave him a hard look. "If he'da called me that just once more," she said, "I think I woulda screamed."

"And I woulda wrapped the rack around his neck. Go ahead Jenny. Wanna get you and your things upstairs so's I c'n go to work."

"And I'll just lay around and get fat."

"If you do, I'll hitch you to the wagon in place o' one o' the horses and let you help haul it for a couple o' hours. Betcha that'll thin you out."

She smiled and led the way through the lobby and up the stairs to her room.

Six

Canavan's first day as Hopewell's sheriff had passed uneventfully. Now it was evening, a minute or so after eight, and Jenny, wearing one of her new dresses, and he were having their supper at the Greek's. Two young men sauntered in, glanced at Canavan but looked interestedly at Jenny who promptly averted their eyes. They seated themselves at a corner table from which they eyed her without Canavan being aware of it. One of them, a stocky, brawny towhead of about twenty or twenty-two, said low-voiced: "She's just my style, Ollie. I could go for her."

His companion, brown-haired and about average-sized, and perhaps a year or two older, grinned. "Never saw a pretty girl who wasn't your style, Howie, or one you couldn't go for."

"This one's different."

"So what?"

"I've gotta find out about her."

"Meaning you're gonna make a play for her?"

"That's the idea," Howie answered. As he saw Nick come toward their table from the kitchen, he said: "Maybe this feller c'n tell me."

Nick halted at their table. "What you wanna eat?"

"Who's the girl?" Howie asked.

The Greek shook his head.

"Mean you don't know?" Howie pressed him.

"No. Him," Nick said, turning slightly and indicating Canavan with a nod. "Him sheriff. Him bad man with gun. Him kill two men last night when they try rob stage company."

"Hell with him," Howie said. "I wanna know about the girl."

"Maybe you wanna go ask sheriff?"

"Don't be so smart," Howie answered curtly.

"What you wanna eat?"

"Looks to me like they're nearly finished," Ollie said.

"They have their coffee yet?" Howie asked Nick.

Nick shook his head.

"Just bring us some apple pie an' coffee."

"Opple pie an' coffee," Nick repeated and trudged back to the kitchen.

The mustached Greek served Canavan and Jenny coffee and pie and followed with the youths' order.

"Let's get done," Howie said. "Wanna get out before they do so's we c'n see where the girl goes."

"Hope we ain't goin' out've our way lookin' for trouble," Ollie said. "I don't like tanglin' with the law, 'specially when the law's so blamed big and handy with his gun."

"I've tangled with even bigger characters than this one," Howie answered, "and made out all right with th'm."

"I know. I was there. Only they were drunks who couldn't hardly stand up, let alone fight back."

"Get done, willya?"

They gulped down their coffee and crammed big

forkfuls of pie into their mouths. Then they got up, grabbed their hats, slapped some coins on the table, and strode out. They found that save for two places, the hotel and Canavan's office whose lights were still burning, the rest of the street was shrouded in deepening darkness.

They took refuge in an alley just beyond the Greek's place and waited. It was so gloomily dark in the alley, neither of them could see the other. Howie peered out guardedly and hastily withdrew his head when he saw Canavan and Jenny coming up the street. When he saw them pass, he peered out again, saw them halt on the walk in front of the hotel and talk briefly. When he saw Canavan turn and cut across the deserted street and head for his office, Howie said to his companion: "Let's go."

"Know where the girl went?"

"Into the hotel."

"And the sheriff?"

"He's in his office. So he's outta the way. So you c'n quit worrying. C'mon."

At Howie's insistence they slipped out of the alley and walking casually and unhurriedly to avoid attracting attention to themselves even though there was no one about, they sauntered into the hotel.

Bick who was behind the counter looked up and nodded. "Evening."

"Evening," the two youths answered.

The towheaded Howie leaned over the counter.

"I'm tryin' to catch up with an old girlfriend o' mine," he told Bick in a confidential tone. "'Less I'm mistaken, I think I saw her comin' in here."

"Oh?" Bick said.

The youth described her.

"Uh-huh," Bick said, nodding. "You've got a

mighty sharp eye, young feller."

"Only one trouble," Howie continued, hunching over on his folded arms. "I dunno what name she's goin' by here. Y'see, she ran away from her husband, a bastid who used to beat hell out of her every time he got a load on and that was just about every day. He's been trailing her ever since. Helluva nice girl and like everyone else who knows her, I'm doggoned sorry for her. Maybe she's runnin' short o' dough. If she is, I'd like to give her some."

"If you wanna leave it here with me, I'll see that she gets it."

Howie pretended to consider Bick's offer. He looked disappointed and finally said: "Now don't get me wrong, Mac. Don't want you to think I don't trust you or anything like that. Only I wanna surprise her."

"Tell me your name," Bick said, "and I'll go ask her if she knows you. If she does, I'll ask her to come downstairs. That's fair enough, isn't it?"

Howie dug in his pants pocket and produced a handful of crumpled up bills, took a five-dollar bill from among them and laid it on the counter, pocketed the other bills, grinned boyishly at Bick and said: "Duplicate keys must cost you anywhere's from a nickel to a dime. I'm willing to pay five bucks for it, giving you a clear profit of four bucks and ninety or ninety-five cents. What do you say? Is it a deal?"

Bick looked at the bill as Howie smoothed it out, then he raised his eyes to meet Howie's.

"Sorry, partner," he said with a shake of his head. "But it's no deal. I'm willing to call her down here if she knows you. But that's it."

Howie's smile and his friendliness vanished. He glanced at Ollie who was standing quietly a couple of steps away. "Keep our friend here company, Ollie. Only keep him covered."

Reluctantly it seemed to Bick, Ollie drew his gun and held it on him.

"Trot out a key to the lady's room, Mac," Howie ordered Bick, "and hurry it."

Bick didn't say anything. He partly opened the drawer under the counter, glanced at the gun that he kept in there together with a box of duplicate keys, put the box on the counter and opened it, and poked around among the keys with his fingers till he found the one that he was looking for, raised his eyes to Howie and held it out to him. "Here y'are. Room 109."

Howie snatched it out of Bick's hand, picked up his five-dollar bill and shoved it into his pocket, turned and headed for the stairs. Ollie turned and followed him with troubled eyes. Unconsciously he lowered his gun. It gave Bick the opportunity he sought.

As Howie topped the stairs and turned on the landing and disappeared from sight, Ollie shook his head and slowly turned around. He stared with wide eyes when he saw the leveled gun in Bick's hand and the muzzle gaping at him hungrily. He gulped and swallowed hard.

"Be smart, young feller," Bick told him quietly, "and put your gun on the counter and get the hell outta here. That's if you wanna go on living. 'Course if you don't. . ."

Bick didn't finish. There was no need. He could see the look of fright in Ollie's eyes, so he knew the cowed youth would obey him. Ollie promptly confirmed his belief. He laid his gun on the counter, stepped back, and started for the doorway when Canavan suddenly appeared in front of him. Recognizing Canavan, and obviously awed by his size, he panicked and hastily backed off from him. Canavan eyed him, then taking his gaze from him for an instant, shot a look at Bick. When he saw the gun in the latter's hand, he looked concerned.

Bick said quickly: "His sidekick's upstairs lookin' for the girl's room."

"Oh?"

"Claims he knows her. But I don't believe him."

"He know where to find her?"

"No. I gave him the key to 109. It won't fit because we've changed the lock. Didn't know what to do 'cept stall him."

"I'll wait for him down here," Canavan said. "You," he said, turning to Ollie, "get down behind the counter with Bick and stay put there. If he lets out one single peep, Bick, wallop him over the head, and good."

Ollie was alive and above everything else he wanted to stay that way. So he needed no urging to obey Canavan. Moving faster than he had ever moved before, he whirled around the counter and dropped down behind it even before Bick did. It took Bick a couple of seconds to grab Ollie's gun off the counter before he dropped to his knees next to the crouching youth.

Loosening his gun in his cutaway holster, Canavan crossed the lobby to the counter, squared himself around and leaned back against it with his elbows resting on the edge of it and the fingers of his hands dangling. There were heavy, scuffing bootsteps overhead. They came rapidly toward the stairs.

Canavan did not turn his gaze on the stairs till he judged Howie to be about halfway down. Then he turned to the youth and said: "Oh! Thought you were the desk clerk. You see 'nything of him?"

Howie frowned. "He was here a minute ago," he replied gruffly.

"Wonder where he went?"

"I wouldn't know," the frustrated youth said.

He came off the stairs, hitched up his pants rather angrily as he came abreast of Canavan, stalked past him and headed for the street. He was within a stride of the open doorway when Canavan came erect and at the same time called: "Hold it a minute, young feller."

Howie stopped, looked back over his thick shoulder, and asked grumpily: "Yeah?"

"What were you doin' upstairs?"

"Lookin' for somebody."

"Like who?"

"For a feller I thought I recognized comin' in here."

"Find him?"

"It wasn't him. It was somebody else who looked something like him."

"You're a liar," Canavan said evenly and Howie bristled. "Unbuckle your gun belt and let it fall."

"Why?"

"Because I said so."

Howie stared hard at him. Then his lip curled a little and he said: "You characters are all alike. Somebody pins a piece o' tin on you and right off you think who the hell you are. You don't mean anything to me, and you don't scare me none."

"Unbuckle your gunbelt and let it fall," Canavan repeated.

Howie grinned evilly. "Maybe you'd like to try an' make me," he said tauntingly.

Canavan took a step toward him. Howie clawed for his gun, came up with it and spun around to shoot. But Canavan who had outdrawn him, outgunned him too. His Colt thundered, and Howie cried out, dropped his gun and clutched his right wrist to him with his left hand. Blood spurted from his wrist and burst through his fingers, drenching them, and ran down the front of him, staining his shirt and pants and puddling his boot-toes.

"You bastid!" he raged at Canavan. "I'll kill you for this!"

He bent over suddenly and sought to pick up his gun

with his bloodied left hand when Canavan leaped at him, applied his right foot to Howie's backside and sent him sprawling on his face. With the same foot, Canavan kicked the youth's gun away. It went slithering across the lobby floor and caroming off the bottom step of the stairway. Pushing himself up from the floor with his left hand and leaving a bloody imprint of his flexed fingers that spanned two boards, Howie got up only to have Canavan fling him around and slam him into the side wall.

"All right, Bick! You c'n come out now!"

Bick promptly stood up. Canavan who had just picked up Howie's gun, shoved it down inside his pants belt. "Be a good feller, Bick, and go fetch the doctor."

"Yeah, sure. Oh, what d'you want me to do with this young feller back here with me?"

"Let him come outta there. I'll keep an eye on him too."

"All right, bucko," Bick said to Ollie. "Up on your feet."

Herding the cowed youth ahead of him at gunpoint, Bick brought him out from behind the counter. Then he retraced his steps, opened the drawer and put his gun away and laid Ollie's next to it. He reached for the opened box of keys, closed it, and put that in the drawer too, and slammed the drawer shut.

As he emerged again, Canavan turned to Ollie and, pointing to the wall opposite the counter, said: "Sit down on the floor against the wall." Ollie hastened to obey. Turning to Howie whose face was contorted with pain, Canavan told him: "Down on the floor next to your partner."

Howie glared at him. "Like I told you before, you bastid," he said thickly, "if it's the last thing I ever do, I'll get you for this."

Canavan leveled a long look at him. "You run off at the mouth. If you don't close it and keep it closed, I'll do it for you. Now get over there."

Howie glowered, but made no attempt to move. Canavan, obviously out of patience with him, caught him by his left arm and with a powerful heave sent him stumbling across the floor. He sprawled over Ollie's feet and fell heavily on his left shoulder, turning himself instinctively to protect his injured arm.

"Goddamn you and your stinkin' big feet!" he yelled at Ollie, livid with rage.

Practically pouncing upon him from behind, Canavan grabbed him by his pants belt and dragged him up, turned him and slammed him into the wall and pushed him down on his backside. Howie shot a look at Ollie who flushed and hastily averted his eyes.

"You yeller-bellied bastid," Howie gritted at him. "How'n hell did I ever let myself get tied up with the likes o' you? You haven't got the guts of a louse. Wanna tell you something, and you'd better hear me good. Stay the hell away from me, or I'll beat your head off."

"Nice, friendly feller, isn't he?" Bick said to Canavan as the latter moved back from his two prisoners.

"Yeah," Canavan answered. "Only where he'll be spending the next couple o'years, he won't have anything to say about who gets put next to him, or about anything else. Go ahead, willya, Bick?"

"On my way," Bick said, and hurried out.

Backed again against the counter with his thumbs hooked in his gunbelt, Canavan was watching his prisoners when he suddenly became aware of wide eyes holding on him. He glanced at the doorway. It was filled to overflowing with townsmen, most of them armed with rifles. The carrying echo of gunfire and their over-powering curiosity to know what had caused the shooting was responsible for their sudden appearance there, he told himself.

There was movement behind them, some pushing and shoving and Canavan heard a familiar voice say, "Lemme through, boys. Lemme through." Al Lennart, rifle-armed like some of the townsmen, shouldered his way through the men crowding the doorway. He stopped a step or two inside the lobby, looked at Canavan, then at the two youths, and again at Canavan. "I dunno what they did, or even what they tried to do. But from the looks of that one," and he jerked his head in Howie's direction, the latter still clutching his injured wrist with his blood-drenched left hand, "I c'n see what you did to him."

"They were looking for trouble and they found it," Canavan said. "Only more than they could handle."

"Uh-huh," Lennart said. "Judge Martin'll be back in a couple o' days and you c'n bring them up before him. Then the marshal who covers this area and who comes through here every five or six weeks is about due, and you can turn them over to him. He'll see to it that they find their way into prison."

"I'd like to see that everything's all right upstairs. You mind keepin' an eye on them for a minute or so?"

"Go right ahead," Lennart told him.

"I sent Bick to fetch the doctor. He oughta be along any minute now."

"Uh-huh," Lennart said again.

Canavan trudged up the stairs. Jenny unlocked and opened her door in answer to his knock and his call. "It's me, Jenny."

"Why didn't you tell me those two young squirts were makin' eyes at you in the Greek's when we were having our supper?'' he wanted to know.

"I didn't pay 'ny attention to them," she replied. "Besides, I didn't want to start 'nything and bring on another scene like I did this morning with that fat drummer. One was enough for today."

"Next time you let me worry about makin' a scene."

"All right, Johnny."

"I wouldn'ta known anything about it if it hadn't been for the Greek. He didn't like the looks o' those two smart alecks, 'specially the light-haired one who has a big mouth. Soon's Nick locked up, he came over to the office and told me. Thought I oughta know. That's what brought me hustlin' over here. To see that you were all right. The big-mouthed one told Bick he knew you and came upstairs lookin' for you. I was waiting for him when he came down. He sassed me and went for his gun only I beat him to the draw. I coulda killed him. Instead I put a bullet through his gunwrist. It'll never be of much use to him again. Now he'll have to learn to do things left-handed."

She had held her gaze on him throughout his recital of what had happened. When she made no comment, he continued. "Lennart's downstairs keepin' his eye on the pair. I sent Bick for the doctor. He's probably here now fixin' up big mouth's wrist."

She looked troubled. "Y'see, Johnny? Why I didn't want to go on with this and why I'd finally made up my mind to go back to Rogers and forget about California? Like I told you, everywhere we go—"

"No," he said firmly. "This was different. It wasn't because somebody's recognized you like that drummer did. This was a case of two young punks who thought they could find you after I left you and make time with you. And that kind o' thing could've happened any-where."

89

"I wish we could get away from here. I don't like this place."

"Don't think I do either. I'm sorry I agreed to stay on, but I promised. But it won't be too long before we pull outta here. I won't let it be. I'll hound Lennart till he grabs the first man who comes along, so's we'll be free to go."

"You have to go back to your office?"

"Yeah, sure. Gotta lock up those two punks. Got a couple o' cells in the cellar under the office. But soon's it gets to be ten o'clock, that'll be it for me. I'll call it a day and lock up. You tired? You wanna get to bed?"

She shook her head. "No. I'll wait till you get back."

"Lock your door," he instructed her.

"No, you do it, and take the key with you."

She took the key out of the lock and gave it to him.

"Watch yourself with those two, Johnny. Those young uns can be awf'lly tricky."

"Don't worry about me. I've hooked up with their kind before. So I know how to deal with th'm." He gave her a reassuring smile and put his hand on the doorknob. "I won't be any longer'n I have to."

As he turned the knob to open the door, she put her hand on his, stopping him. He turned questioning eyes on her. "S'matter?"

"Nothing," she said and took her hand away. "Go do what you have to and come back here."

He gave her a wondering look. She turned away from him. "What's bothering you, Jenny?"

"Nothing," she flung at him over her shoulder. "Go do what you have to."

He was motionless for a moment. Then he closed and locked the door. Pocketing the key, he went downstairs. Lennart and two townsmen, all of them with their rifles on the two youths, were backed against the counter while Bick, who had returned, was behind it. The doctor with his opened kit on the floor was kneeling at Howie's side and bandaging his right wrist. Everyone except the doctor looked around at Canavan.

"Howie glared at him. "Lousy bastid," he fairly spat at Canavan. "Why didn't you kill me instead o' crippling me?"

"Maybe I shoulda," Canavan answered. "I coulda easy enough. That woulda been one sure way of shutting your mouth."

The doctor had finished his bandaging. Now he fashioned a sling out of a piece of white cloth, secured the ends of it behind Howie's neck and gently eased the youth's arm into it. He closed his bag and stood up. Turning to Lennart, he said: "Think I'd better have a look at that arm daily for the next couple of days.

Lennart indicated Canavan with a nod and the doctor looked at him.

"You can see him any time you like," Canavan said simply.

The doctor grunted, picked up his bag, and turned to go. The men who were still crowding the doorway moved as he came toward them, opening a path for him, and he went out. Promptly, though, the path closed again.

"All right," Canavan said to Ollie and Howie. "Up on your feet."

Ollie got up at once, by himself. Howie seemed to experience some difficulty, so Canavan gave him a hand and hauled him to his feet, ignoring the hard look the youth gave him.

"Sheriff," Bick said and beckoned. Canavan leaned over the counter and listened to Bick's account of what had happened prior to Canavan's sudden return to the hotel. "That's it," Bick said. "Thought you oughta know."

Canavan nodded. "You took an awful chance with

these two smark alecks. Glad I got here in time to make sure that nothing happened to you."

Bick grinned. "So am I."

Turning around again, Canavan said: "All right, you two. Let's go."

"Just a minute now," Howie said. "Just what are you takin' us in for? What'd we do aside from makin' the mistake of comin' into this lousy town?"

"If you don't know, and if you can't figure it out for yourself, then I'm sorry for you because you're even more stupid than I thought," Canavan replied. "So you wait till you come up in court. The judge'll be only too glad to tell you."

"And how he will!" Lennart chimed in. "He's old and crotchety, and if there's anything he hates it's a smart aleck. He'll give you everything the law says he c'n, and then just for good measure, he'll add a little on his own."

"Let's go," Canavan said, as he herded his prisoners ahead of him.

The path that had opened earlier for the doctor opened again, a little wider this time to permit the two youths and their captor to make their way out to the street. Canavan guided them across the darkened street and into his office. Lennart followed them and, closing the door behind him, stood backed against it with his rifle cradled in his arms.

Thumbing his hat up from his forehead, Canavan seated himself at his desk, picked up a stub of a pencil, and reached for a blank piece of paper. "You," he said to Ollie. "What's your name, how old are you and where d'you come from?"

"Ollie Phelps, I'm twenty-three and I hail from Kansas," was the reply.

"Whereabouts in Kansas?"

"Rocky Pass."

Canavan noted the information on the paper and lifted his eyes to Howie.

"All right," he said briskly. "Let's have it. Name, age, and where you come from."

"I'm not tellin' you a damned thing," Howie said spitefully.

"If that's the way you want it, it's all right with me," Canavan answered calmly. "Only I hope you don't get too hungry before you change your mind about talking because you're not gonna get anything to eat or drink till then."

He rose and opened the door that led to the sheriff's living quarters, crossed the room to still another door, opened that one, and went down a short flight of stairs, his bootheels thumping on the steps. When he returned a couple of minutes later, he held the connecting door wide and said curtly: "C'mon."

Ollie moved without delay, Howie a little reluctantly. Lennart following them with his eyes, saw them with Canavan dogging their bootsteps go down the stairs. He heard an iron door open and slam shut and heard a key grate in the lock. The same procedure was repeated a moment later. Then Canavan reappeared, closed the connecting door behind him and put a big iron key in the top desk drawer.

"That's that," he announced.

Lennart nodded, turned and stepping back, opened the street door and sauntered out. Canavan turned out the light in the lamp that hung from a short piece of chain from a rafter directly above his desk, followed Lennart out to the street, and yanked the door shut and locked it.

"Guess I c'n go turn in now," Lennart said, hoisting his rifle and slinging it across his shoulder.

Canavan nodded. "Thanks for your help."

"G'wan," Lennart retorted, leading the way across the street. "All I did was stick my nose in where it wasn't needed. Far as I could see you had everything under control. So the last thing you needed was help from anybody and that included me. Y'know, just watchin' you, the way you did things, I learned something that's gonna make it tough on the man who takes over from you. I know what to expect from him. So he'll have to measure up, or we'll keep lookin' around for somebody to replace him."

"I sure hope you get somebody real soon," Canavan said. "I'm getting itchier every day to get going."

"Uh-huh. Well, let's see what tomorrow brings us. Maybe somebody who's had experience and who's lookin' for a lawman's job will come wandering in."

"I'd like that to happen."

"Doesn't cost 'nything to hope, y'know."

"I know, and I'm hoping right along with you."

They stepped up on the walk in front of the hotel. The doorway was empty. The townsmen, their curiosity satisfied, had returned to their homes.

"See you tomorrow, Canavan."

"Right."

The lobby floor was wet, proof that Bick had mopped it, removing traces of the blood that Howie had left behind him. The lobby itself was deserted and the counter unmanned. Just as Lennart would do shortly, Bick had already turned in. Canavan tramped up the stairs, halted in front of Jenny's room, fished in his pocket for her key, found it and unlocked her door. He poked his head in. The lamp on Jenny's bureau showed only the barest bit of light burning in it, leaving most of the room in shadowy darkness. She hadn't waited for him to return. She had gone to bed. She lay on her side, her back turned to the door. He glided in, quietly closed the door, and tiptoed across the uncovered floor. He frowned when a board creaked under his foot. He came up to the bed, bent over and peered closely at Jenny.

"Jenny," he breathed at her.

Without opening her eyes she mumbled: "Go 'way. I'm tired and I wanna sleep."

"All right," he said, straightening up. "I'll see you tomorrow."

"That'll be nice," she said sarcastically. "I c'n hardly wait."

He frowned again. "S'matter with you? What's eating you?"

"I told you I'm tired and I wanna sleep, didn't I?"

He made no response. He turned on his heel and went striding out. He yanked the door shut behind him, locked it, and, kneeling in front of it, pushed the key under the door.

Seven

It was the next day, the time about noon. Considerably more thoughtful-looking than usual, but with an air of impatience about him, Canavan was idling in the open doorway of his office. While he kept shifting his gaze about over the street, most of the time it was focused on the window in Jenny's room. The fact that the shade was fully drawn meant that she was still asleep. It irked him because this was one morning when he had hoped that she would get up at a reasonably early hour. They had things to discuss and matters to settle between them, and the sooner they got to them and talked them out, the better he would like it. Her unexplained, and as far as he was concerned uncalled for, change in manner the previous night had given him cause for concern. While he was annoyed with her, and disappointed in her too, he did not deny himself that he would be even more disappointed if she decided at the last moment not to accompany him to California.

"I'd be lyin' to myself if I tried to make myself believe that I don't want her or need her when I know damned well that I do," he thought to himself. "So even though she isn't the kind o' girl I'd go after ordinarily, and the fact that she's quick tempered and she's got a sharp tongue, I'm willing to make allowances. Only thing that makes me leery about her is her on-again, off-again moods. That's why I think we'd better do us some plain talking and settle things between us once an' for all. If she's gonna go on gettin' her back up every little while, the deal between us is off." Suddenly he saw the shade over her window go up. "She must be dressed," he said half-aloud. "So she oughta be coming out any minute now."

He fixed his gaze on the hotel doorway. Several long minutes passed before she appeared. She emerged, crossed the walk to the curb, and waited there till a buckboard with a man and a bonneted woman riding in it rumbled by. Then, lifting her full skirts, she crossed the street, and, again raising her skirts, stepped up on the walk. She halted and looked at Canavan, obviously waiting for him to join her. A couple of townspeople, a woman going down the street and a man heading in the opposite direction, glanced at her as they came abreast of her. She ignored them. Canavan stepped outside, yanked the door shut, and strode over to her. There was no exchange of greetings.

"You mind eating in here?" he asked, nodding in the direction of the lunchroom which was just beyond them.

She turned her head. "Up to you."

"Handier to the office."

"Then by all means let's eat here."

He followed her into the lunchroom, helped her seat herself on one of the stools, straddled the one next to hers, and put his hat on the stool next to him.

"I'm sorry about last night, Johnny," she said.

"So am I. You mind telling me what got you so het up at me?"

"It wasn't you. It was me. I was outta sorts." When

97

he made no comment, she continued. "I haven't anything to do with myself and that's not good. I lay around waiting for you to get back—and with nothing to do but think, I get the craziest ideas. It's stupid of me, I know. But I can't help it. Do you honestly think we'll ever get away from here? I've put all my hopes in California, and in you, but somehow I get the feeling that it'll never be. That it isn't meant to be. That in the end you'll stay put here, and I'll wind up back in Rogers' place. So I get feeling low. And when I take it out on you, even though I don't mean to, I feel twice as bad. Maybe you oughta let me go back where I came from, and you stay put here, or go on your way alone? It'll be easier on you either way without having me around to make trouble for you. What d'you think, Johnny? Be honest with me." Before he could answer, she said low-voiced: "We're getting company. Lennart and another man."

Canavan who had just hunched over the edge of the counter on his folded arms, straightened up, and turned his head toward the door. Lennart, followed by a tall, lean, sun-bronzed man who wore his gun the way Canavan did, low-slung and thong-tied around his right thigh, came up to him. Lennart smiled at Jenny and lifted his hat to her while the man with him took off his hat and held it in his hands.

"Canavan, I'd like you to know Dan Peeples."

Canavan who had already gotten to his feet shook hands with the newcomer.

"Dan't just quit sheriffing over at High Mount," Lennart said. "After eight years there, he thinks he c'n do with a change o' people and scenery. He's ready to take over from you right now, or whenever you say the word."

Canavan grinned. "Right now's good with me."

He unpinned his star and handed it to Lennart who pinned it to the flap of Peeples' shirt pocket.

"So you're your own man again," Lennart said to Canavan. "How soon d'you figure you'll be pulling out?"

"Soon's I made a deal with the stableman for one o' his spare wagons," Canavan replied.

"Uh-huh. Will you come over to the office after a while and help me get Dan started?"

"Yeah, sure," Canavan said. "Say in about an hour or so?"

"Fine," Lennart answered. "We'll be looking for you."

Peeples followed him out. Canavan seated himself again, looked at Jenny, and asked: "Well? What've you got to say now?"

"I'm awf'lly glad, Johnny. But at the same time I'm ashamed of myself for letting myself think those foolish things. I should have known better."

"Forget it. What d'you wanna eat?"

"Funny thing. But when we came in here, I wasn't at all hungry. Now, all of a sudden, I'm starved."

"Once I know we've got a wagon, I'll go get stocked up on grub and everything else we might need. Meantime if there's anything you might want, get it while the getting's good. We won't be hitting any towns, y'know. We'll be keeping to the open country."

"You planning to pull out today?"

"'Course. Why wait around and lose time when he c'n be putting distance between us and Hopewell? So soon's we finish eating, get yourself packed up. My stuff's ready. All I have to do is grab it. I'll see Bick and get squared away with him for both of us."

"I'll be ready to go when you are."

At three that afternoon, with the mare, Willie, tied to

the tailgate of their wagon, and protesting nasally because she felt that Canavan was neglecting her by driving the wagon when he should have been riding her, they left Hopewell and took the road west.

"Nothing to it," Canavan said to Jenny. "Just play out the lines so that the horses won't fight you when they wanna run. Same time though see that you have a good grip on the lines in case you think they're running too fast and you wanna slow th'm down. Wanna give it a try?"

"Yes."

He passed her the reins and she got a secure grip on them. She watched the horses continue their pace without breaking stride and looked at Canavan. "They don't even know I'm doing the driving now."

"No." She drove on and after a while, he said: "Pull up so's I c'n get down."

She obeyed, bringing the team and the wagon to a full stop. One of the horses looked around at her.

Canavan climbed down, and shifting his holster a little bit, disappeared around the back of the wagon. He reappeared shortly astride Willie and ranged up alongside of Jenny. "All right. Go ahead," he said.

She jerked the reins and the horses trotted away. "I like that Lennart man, Johnny," she said, "and Bick too."

"Both o' th'm are good men in my book. Lennart gave me a whole week's wages even though I didn't have anywhere near that much coming to me. Twenty-five bucks and one o' the horses went to the stableman for the wagon and the harness. So actually it wasn't anything out've my pocket that swung the deal for us."

"Uh-huh," she said, easing up a little on the lines. The horses, obviously eager to run, promptly quickened their pace. "Lennart gave me such a warm handshake and wished us all the best, and Bick made such a to-do outta saying goodbye to me, they made me feel good all over. Oh, what about those two smart alecks? What happens to them now?"

"I gave Peeples the story on them. Soon's that judge gets back, Peeples will bring them up before him."

"I see. Hey, how am I doing?"

"Fine. Like you've been driving a team all your life."

She laughed lightly. He eyed her. She was brighter than he had ever seen her before. She was happy that at long last they were on their way.

"How long d'we keep going?" she wanted to know.

"Till around sundown. Then we'll make camp and have us something to eat, and after a while we'll turn in. Wanna get us an early start tomorrow morning. Cover more ground before noon than y'do in the afternoon. By then the sun gets hot and the horses, having been on the go for hours, feel it, so you don't make any time worth talking about. So it's how far you get by noon that really counts."

"Oh," she said. "How long d'you figure it'll take us to get to California?"

"Somewhere's around four weeks. Depends of course on the weather. If we get bogged down by rain and mud, it'll take even longer."

There was little conversation between them after that. Time and distance dropped away from them. Save for the jingle of the harness, the creak of the wagon, the cutting spin of the big wheels and the rhythmic beat of the horses' hoofs, silence hung over the open country. It was as though they were the only ones abroad in that vast expanse of prairie land. Once though when they came within a mile or so of a house from whose chimney smoke was lifting lazily into the late afternoon sky, Jenny couldn't take her eyes from it. Canavan noticed but made no comment.

"People living alone out here in the middle of nowhere," he heard her say, and he raised his eyes to her. "Wonder how they like it?" When he offered no opinion, she continued. "I suppose they must like it or they wouldn't stay put. Right?"

"Right."

" 'Course if they get along, they don't need 'nybody else. With the man working the place and keeping busy at it all day and the woman just as busy with her chores, time oughtn't hang heavy on their hands. And if they have a couple o' kids, watching them grow up oughta help make life interesting for th'm."

"It isn't an easy life, Jenny. Fact is, it's a hard life."

"What kind isn't?" she countered.

He made no attempt to answer her question. Instead he asked: "Think you'd like that kind o' life? Don't you think you'd get fed up with it after a while and want out of it?"

She thought about it briefly before she replied.

"Nope," she said frankly. "I kinda think I'd like it. I've had enough excitement to last me a long, long time. So I think I'd like a change. The kind o' life those people over there must live. What about you, Johnny?"

"Well, like you, I've had my share of excitement, and I don't need any more. I'd like to have a place of my own again. Only I wouldn't want it out here, away from the rest o' the world. I'd like it fairly close to a town, and the smaller the town the better I'd like it. And with nice, decent, friendly people in it."

"Uh-huh," she said. "And what about the kids?"

He grinned at her. "I like kids, and all kinds o' th'm too. Fact is, I'd always hoped I'd have a flock o' th'm. Something of my folks musta rubbed off on me because they had six."

"And mine had one. Me."

He ranged his gaze around and looked skyward. Longfingered shadows were beginning to drape themselves over the prairie.

She looked about. "We've been jawin' away like a couple o' good fellers. So we didn't notice it was getting dark. Leastways, I didn't."

"Yeah, be evening soon," Canavan said. "Think we'll make camp right here. "Pull up, Jenny, and turn inland."

Again she followed his instructions, slowed the team to a walk, and followed him up a slight embankment and on some twenty or thirty feet beyond. She halted the horses when he wheeled around and held up his hand.

"Pull back hard on the handbrake," he called to her, "and loop the lines around it and slip-knot th'm."

"Right," she said, did as he told her to. "Anything else?"

"Nope. That's it."

She stood up and waited. He dismounted and came to her, held up his arms for her and she came to him, curling both arms around his neck. He lifted her clear of the front left wheel and turned with her. But instead of letting him set her down on the ground, she clung to him and kissed him hard on the mouth.

"Now don't ask me what that was for," she said. "I kissed you because I wanted to. That a good enough reason?"

He grinned at her. "I can't think of a better one."

With her arms still encircling his neck and their faces but an inch or two apart, she said: "Y'know something? Outside o' that one peck you gave me the night Lennart came upstairs to proposition you to stay on in Hope-well, you've never kissed me just like that, or even made

103

'ny move to. You afraid o' me, Johnny? Afraid you're liable to catch something from me if you let yourself go with me?''

"No, 'course not.''

"Are you afraid I'll think you're taking advantage of me and that I'll let out a big holler?''

"Nope."

"Then what is it?" she pressed him. "Is it on account o' Beth? If it is, then you oughta know you can't go on the rest o' your life makin' out she's still alive and waiting for you to come back to her when she's been dead an' gone for years."

"Beth hasn't anything to do with it."

"Then what has?" she asked him. "Wait up now. I know what you think o' women who work in saloons. Is it because o' that, that I was one o' th'm and you can't let yourself forget that, that you're willing to help me get to California, but that's all, and that that's why you've been keeping your distance from me?''

"You know how fond I am of you, Jenny.''

"Being fond o' me is fine for a starter. But can't you do a little better than that? If you'd let yourself go, you might be surprised to find yourself feeling about me the way I do about you. Y'know, when I talked you into agreeing to take me out to California with you, all I wanted was to get out there. Then I'd go off on my own. But things have changed since then. Leastways they have with me. Maybe I shouldn't tell you this. But I'm hoping that by the time we get there, you'll be so used to having me around, you won't wanna let me go. That you'll wanna keep me around for always.''

"Could be. Now lemme ask your something.''

"Go ahead. Ask me anything you like.''

"When you say that things have changed with you since then, what's that supposed to mean? You tryin' to tell me you're in love with me?"

"What d'you think, you big ox?" she demanded. "Who's been taking care o' me and lookin' out for me ever since you hauled me outta that busted-down stage? Or if you wanna go back to the day before that, to that time in the hotel when that scurvy lookin' bum came barging in on me when I was changing my dress, who'd I come running to and who saved me from him? And who was willing to stake me to a ticket to California and do something extra to keep me going when I got there when there wasn't any call for you to do that like I was your responsibility? And who's always treated me like I was a somebody, and who kept me going whenever I got feeling low and sorry for myself? You, that's who. 'Course I love you, you big redheaded ox. After all you've done for me, even if I hadn'ta wanted to fall for you, d'you think I coulda stopped myself? I'd have had to be made o' stone instead o' flesh an' blood."

There was a sudden, startling sound of whimpering somewhere beyond them yet close by in the rapidly deepening shadows. Then there was movement in the lush grass that carpeted the area.

"What's that?" Jenny breathed at Canavan.

"I dunno. But I'm gonna find out. Look, you get up in the wagon and stay put there till I get back." He turned with her, again lifted her clear of the wheel and helped her reach the driver's seat. "Climb down inside," he told her. "There are a couple o' lanterns under the seat. Gimme one o' th'm."

She followed his instructions, swung around over the seat and climbed down into the body of the wagon, and disappeared. But she reappeared almost at once.

"Here," she said in a low, guarded voice. "But be careful, Johnny."

She passed him a lantern. He knelt down with it next

to the wagon. She heard a match strike, and presently saw light flame in the grass. Peering out she saw him put the lighted lantern on the ground a dozen feet or so from the wagon and saw him move hastily away from it and crouch down in the grass. He would be out of the circle of light that the lantern cast off and safely within the shadows while whoever was coming toward the wagon would be in the light. The whimpering was a little louder as it came closer and so was the movement in the grass. Then she heard Canavan's voice.

"Well, hello there, young lady. You looking for someone?"

Craning her neck, Jenny stared with widening eyes when she saw the figure of a little girl come into view, and saw Canavan on his knees in front of her.

"We've got company, Jenny," she heard him call. "Come on out here and have a look."

"Coming," she answered. Hastily she hoisted herself up on the seat and swung herself over it. Moments later she was kneeling at Canavan's side and looking wonderingly at the little girl who was sniffling and in turn looking wide-eyed at them. "Where's your mother, honey?" Jenny asked.

"She's still sleeping," was the reply. "I couldn't wake her up. When it got dark, I got frightened and I didn't know what to do."

"You poor darling," Jenny said and held out her arms to her. The child came to her quite willingly and Jenny comforted her. "We'll take you back to your mother. But don't cry. There's nothing to be scared of now."

"Will you wake Mama up and tell her I'm awful hungry?"

"Yes, honey," Jenny assured her. Then turning to

Canavan she asked: "Johnny, think you can. . .?"

"I'll get her something she can eat while we're taking her back," he said, getting up on his feet.

He strode back to the wagon. When he returned some minutes later, Jenny was sitting in the grass wth the little girl in her lap. Jenny lifted her eyes to him.

"Her name is Dora May Cole," she told him gravely. "But Mama calls her Dolly."

"Uh-huh," Canavan said. "Here y'are, Dora May." He held out something to the child. "A nice, fresh sugar bun and it's all for you."

"Thank you," she said with surprising graciousness. She took the bun from him and bit into it and promptly added: "This is good. Can I have another one?"

Canavan knelt down again and laughed. "Soon's you finish the one you're eating now."

The first bun was quickly devoured. The child was eating the second one when Canavan helped Jenny to her feet. But she refused to put the little girl down and insisted upon carrying her. With Canavan holding the lantern high and leading the way, they started off in the direction in which Dora May had come. It took him fully half an hour before he spied the rounded, upper structure of a full-sized Conestoga looming up in the night light. Halting in front of it and ignoring the whinnies of a team of horses that were standing in the traces, Canavan, with the lantern swinging from his hand and the turned-up light playing over the high step, hauled himself up to the driver's seat and called out: "Mrs. Cole!"

There was no response, no sound either from inside the big wagon.

Maneuvering himself over the wide seat, Canavan climbed down into the wagon. Raising the lantern, he played the light over its interior and contents. It was loaded with furniture, big, heavy pieces as well as many smaller ones. A narrow aisle that was flanked by furniture and ran the length of the wagon held his eye for in it, stretched out on the flat of her back on a doubled-over blanket, lay a fully dressed woman. Canavan knelt at her side. "Mrs. Cole."

Holding the lantern just above her so that the light shone on her face, he watched her closely for a couple of moments, and finally bent low over her. Then slowly, grim-looking, he eased back on his haunches, and presently stood up, made his way forward again to the driver's seat, tugged at the canvas curtain that hung behind the seat and freeing it, let it drop. Minutes later he was standing at Jenny's side. She leveled anxious eyes at him.

"I think we'd better let her sleep on," he said, more for the child's benefit than for Jenny's, "and not try to wake her tonight. She must be very tired. Tomorrow morning right after breakfast we'll come back here. All right?"

Jenny answered for Dora May as well as for herself.

"I think that's a very good idea," she said. "Dora May can sleep in our wagon tonight. Would you like that, honey?" she asked the child.

"I—I guess so," was the somewhat hesitant reply. "If you think Mama will think it's all right."

"Oh, I'm sure she will," Jenny assured her. Then turning to Canavan, she asked: "We go back now?"

"In a minute. Wanna unhitch the horses and tie th'm up to the wagon. Give th'm a little more freedom and a little more room to move around in."

While Jenny held the lantern, Canavan unharnessed the horses and tied each to a big wheel. Then taking the lantern from Jenny, he said: "If she gets too much for you, lemme know and I'll spell you."

"My arm's a little tired now. If you'd like to take her for a while. . ."

He handed the lantern back to her and held out his arms to Dora May.

"How about a ride on my shoulders?" he asked her. When she leaned toward him, he lifted her, turned her and seated her astride his shoulders, and turning his head, asked her: "How's that, all right? Comf'table?"

"Oh, yes!" Dora May answered quickly. "This is fun."

This time Jenny took the lead, holding the lantern aloft so that Canavan, trudging along at her heels, could see where he was going. Once or twice he sagged deliberately and promptly came erect, jouncing the child, and she laughed. The darkness, continuing to deepen, lay over the far-flung land like an obscuring blanket. They went on in silence after that, till Jenny happened to turn and look back. Then she said in a guarded tone: "She's asleep, Johnny."

He stopped and reached up and eased the child off his shoulders and, cradling her in his arms, tramped on after Jenny. When they came up to their wagon, Jenny climbed up and Canavan handed her the little girl, then while Jenny waited with her, he hoisted himself up too, swung over the seat and dropped down into the wagon. Jenny heard him moving about and wondered what he was doing, and just as she was about to turn her head and call to him, he reappeared and held up his arms for Dora May. Following his instructions, Jenny managed to ease herself down into the wagon too.

"I've opened my bedroll," he told Jenny. "Lay her in that after you get her things off."

109

While he held the child, Jenny undressed her, and while she laid Dory May in the bedroll and covered her up, Canavan busied himself at the rear of the wagon. When he rejoined her, he said: "Laid out the mattress and the blanket we're gonna use. You hungry?"

"No, not very. Fact is, a cup o' coffee would do me fine. Y'got any more o' those sugar buns left? You know, for Dora May when she wakes up."

"Got a whole bagful. All that lunchroom feller had. Think he said there were twenty-six all told."

"Think I could go one o' them with the coffee."

Some twenty minutes later, as they were sitting cross-legged in the grass near the wagon with the lantern on the ground just beyond them, drinking the freshly boiled coffee and each munching a bun, Jenny put down her cup. "Poor kid. She doesn't know what she's in for without her mother to take care o' her and look out for her. I know what it's like, and you c'n take my word for it it's lousy. What are we gonna do about her, Johnny?"

"Can't leave her here and with nobody around for us to turn her over to, looks to me like the only thing we can do is lug her along with us."

"Uh-huh," she said, raising her cup to her lips.

"Tomorrow morning I'll bury her mother. We'll take the horses. Y'never know what c'n happen to the ones we've got and it's nice to know we've got a couple o' spares just in case. But we'll leave the wagon. Anybody who comes along and wants it and the stuff in it c'n have it."

They finished drinking their coffee in silence. When he took her cup from her and got up, she arose too and said:

"I'm kinda beat, Johnny. So if it's all right with you, I think I'll go turn in."

"Go ahead. Got a few things to do before I c'n turn in. But it shouldn't take me long."

"Careful when you climb up so's you don't wake Dora May."

"I'll watch it."

She turned toward the wagon, stopped and said over her shoulder: "Chances are I'll be asleep by the time you're set to turn in. So I'd better say goodnight to you now."

He put down the cups and came to her, gripped her by the arms, bent his head and kissed her full on the lips.

"G'night, Jenny," he said, releasing her.

"G'night, Johnny," she responded. "That was nice. Like you really meant it."

"I did mean it."

"That makes it even nicer."

The cups and the coffeepot had been rinsed out, the fire stamped out and covered with scooped-up dirt, Willie unsaddled and tied to a rear wheel on one side of the wagon and the team unhitched and tied to a wheel on the other side when Canavan finally hauled himself up into the wagon. Turning down the lantern light till only the barest glow burned in it, he removed his boots, tiptoed around the sleeping child and made his way to where Jenny lay blanketed on the mattress. Her dress, he noticed, lay on top of two large gunny sacks of food-stuffs. He turned out the light and put the lantern on the floor, and laid his rolled-up gunbelt next to it and within easy reach. He took off his shirt and draped it over a sack of potatoes and started to take off his pants. He stopped and looked thoughtfully in Jenny's direction. As though he were a young bridegroom about to get into bed for the first time with his newly acquired bride, he seemed hesitant and shy. But then he pulled off his pants and slung them across his shirt, lifted the blanket and quietly got in under it.

"Johnny," Jenny whispered, startling him.

He jerked his head around to her.

"S'matter?" he asked her. "Thought you were asleep."

"I waited for you to come to bed so's I could ask you something."

"Oh? What is it?"

"I don't want Dora May to hear me. Can't you move a little closer to me?" He moved himself closer to her. "That's better," she said. "Johnny, can't we keep her?"

"Y'sure you want her? Mean a lot o' work for you taking care of a sprout like her, y'know."

"I know, and I'm willing. But it's up to you."

"If you want her that bad, we'll keep her."

"Thanks, Johnny."

"For what? She's a cute kid, so I'll enjoy her as much as you will."

For a while after that they lay quietly, probably no more than six inches apart. A couple of times he started to move even closer to her. But each time he stopped himself, and each time he promptly berated himself. There was an invisible barrier between them that he couldn't seem to surmount despite his longing for her. It was Johnny who helped bridge the space between them when she moved even closer to him so that their shoulders touched.

"Funny, isn't it, how things happen?" she whispered.

"How d'you mean?"

"For years you were a loner. Then you met up with me, did me as good turn and followed that up by just about saving my life. So I paid you back by latching on to you." She moved again, this time so that her head was against his shoulder with the fragrance of her hair

112

lifting into his face. "Now that we're gonna keep Dora May, you've got yourself a family. Funny, isn't it? Proves you never know what's gonna happen next."

Before he could answer, Willie suddenly whinnied, and Canavan lay motionlessly, listening intently. When the mare snorted and whinnied again, louder this time than before, Canavan told Jenny: "Stay put. Something's goin' on outside and I'd better go see what it is."

"You hafta?" Jenny wanted to know a little crossly.

He didn't answer, but simply kicked off the cover, reached for his pants and drew them on, pulled on his boots, fumbled around for his gunbelt and drew his gun. He tiptoed to the rear of the wagon, quietly untied the drop curtain, lifted a corner of it and stole a guarded look outside. Despite the obscuring and somewhat distorting darkness, he managed to make out the figures of two men, one of them mounted, the other one on foot. The latter was trying to untie Willie. When she snorted and shied away from him and rearing up, suddenly lashed out at him with her fore hoofs, he backed off in alarm.

"Aw, c'mon, willya, Mack?" Canavan heard the mounted man say. "We're wastin' time here. You lookin' to get us caught?"

"How long d'you think that plug o' yours is gonna carry the two of us?" the man named Mack retorted. "I want a horse o' my own and this one looks like the kind I've always wanted. So I aim to have her."

Again he sought to grab Willie's bridle, and again she lashed out at him.

Quietly Canavan climbed over the tailgate and ease himself down to the ground. Inching his way around the back of the wagon, he stepped out boldly with his gun leveled. "Reach, you buzzards, or I'll shoot," he said evenly.

The mounted man flung his horse around, lashed him and sent him pounding away. Canavan ignored him and held his gaze on his companion. The man cursed and backed off a step or two. When his right arm jerked, a sign that he was going for his gun, Canavan shot him. The man gasped when the bullet, fired at such close range, slammed into him, robbed him of his breath. He sagged and fell against the wagon and crumpled up in the grass in a broken heap.

Eight

It was some ten minutes later when Canavan climbed back into the wagon. As he eased himself over the tailgate and stepped down on the floor, the lantern flamed, lighting up the interior of the wagon. Jenny, who was wearing her kimona over her nightdress, hastily lowered the light, twisted around and caught up a rifle that lay across the heaped-up blanket on the mattress.

"Oh!" she said when she saw him. There was relief in her voice. "You all right?"

"Yeah, sure," he answered. "Where'd you get that," he asked, pointing to the rifle, "and what were you gonna do with it?"

"I was gonna go see what was keeping you. I remembered seeing a couple o' rifles laying under the seat when I fished out that lantern for you. So I grabbed up one o' th'm. That shooting I heard—"

"There was only one shot. Some highbinder was trying to untie Willie and make off with her."

"And you chased him away."

"No. I had to put a slug in him." He held out his hand for the rifle. She gave it to him and he propped it up in the corner of the wagon where the tailgate and the side wall of the wagon came together at right angles to each other. "I dragged him away from the wagon and dumped him in some tall grass. Didn't want you or Dora May to see him layin' right outside when you came out for breakfast. Then I had to calm down Willie."

"I'm glad that's all there was to it. You're gonna hafta be awf'lly careful from now on. You can't afford to take chances. You've got responsibilities, y'know."

He grinned at her. "Y'mean I've got me a family to look out for?"

She smiled back at him apologetically and said: "I'm afraid so, Johnny. I know you weren't lookin' to be saddled with one. But you are. Aren't you sorry you ever took up with me?"

"Nope. G'wan back to bed."

"What are you gonna do?"

"Go back to bed too."

When he rejoined her under the blanket and reached out for her to bring her into his arms, she whispered: "Wait, Johnny. You doing this because it's what you want, or because you think it's what I want you to do?"

"It's what I want."

He was up again at dawn and, carrying his boots, managed to climb out of the wagon without waking either Jenny or Dora May. There was only the barest bit of light in the sky. The air was dampish and uncomfortably chilly. Suddenly remembering that he needed a shovel for the unpleasant task that awaited him, he climbed up again and groped around under the seat till he found what he was looking for.

It was forty minutes later when he returned, driving the dead woman's team ahead of him with the lines and the shovel gripped in his left hand and a cloth-covered box similar to Jenny's on his right shoulder. The spare horses were unhitched and tied to the tailgate, the shovel with bits of sweet-smelling, freshly turned earth clinging to it was propped up against the wagon while the box that held Dora May's clothes rested on the wide seat of the wagon. He had just finished building a fire and was about to boil water for coffee when the drop curtain behind the seat was pushed aside and Jenny poked her head out at him.

"Johnny!" she called.

He strode over to the wagon and lifted his eyes to her. "Dory May and I could use some hot water."

"Gimme a couple o' minutes and you c'n have it."

Jenny withdrew her head and the curtain dropped back in place and hung motionlessly. The hot water was forthcoming shortly, poured into a second pot from the coffeepot. Then more water was boiled. When coffee was spooned into it, the beans promptly dissolved and almost at once a rich, tempting fragrance began to lift and fill the early morning air. The light in the sky, Canavan had already noticed had brightened while the damp chill that had greeted him when he had climbed down earlier was gone. It would be a pleasant day, he told himself after another skyward glance.

"Oughta be able to make time today," he muttered. "Gotta take advantage of every good day that comes along because there'll be plenty o' bad ones in b'tween."

"Johnny!"

Again he strode over to the wagon. The box had been removed. As before, Jenny's head was poked out at him.

"Yeah?" he asked her.

"Dora May's papa is in heaven," she told him gravely. "I've told her that her mama's gone there too, to join him, and that from now on Dora May's gonna be our little girl.''

"Right.''

"She's ready for breakfast. Will you take her, please?''

"Yeah, sure,'' he replied and hauled himself up to the seat and held out his arms to the child when Jenny lifted her onto it. "My,'' he said, "aren't we lucky to have such a pretty little girl for our own?''

Dora May managed a wan little smile. However her eyes showed that she had been crying. He lifted her off the seat, settled her securely within the hollow of his left arm, and climbed down with her. He carried her over to the fire and seated her on his saddle that he had dragged out from under the wagon and had brought over for her to sit on. When Jenny hoisted herself up from the body of the wagon and onto the seat, Canavan hurried over and held up his arms to her. She came to him and he lifted her clear of the right front wheel and set her down on the ground.

As she smoothed down her dress over her hips, she said: "I liked being kissed goodnight. Think I'd like being kissed good morning, too.''

"Oh, you would, huh?'' he said with a grin and kissed her. "You one o' those, what d'they call 'em, creatures of habit?''

"Uh-huh. And when it's such a nice habit, I'm all for it. You mind?''

"Nope. Fact is, I like it too.''

When he held out his hand to her, she took it and squeezed it, and let him lead her over to the fire. Dora May moved and made room for her too on the saddle.

"Don't you think she's a good size for four an' a half?'' Jenny asked Canavan.

"Uh-huh. And about as pretty a young un as any I've

118

ever seen. She'll be a real heart breaker when she grows up."

"I think so too. But I don't think I'll look that far ahead just yet. Oh, and she drinks coffee when there isn't any milk."

Canavan filled two cups and handed one to Jenny, the other one to Dora May and then brought each of them a bun. He filled a third cup for himself and eased himself down in the grass with it and sat cross-legged and lifted it to his lips. Suddenly Willie whinnied and Canavan and Jenny looked up, the latter apprehensively.

"Somebody coming?" she asked.

He nodded, put down his cup and got to his feet. He stood motionlessly for a moment or so, then he turned and looked in a northwesterly direction. Jenny stood up too and ranged her gaze after his. But after a moment or so, when she could neither see nor hear anything to confirm Willie's warning, he said: "There they are, Jenny. See th'm?"

She stared with wide eyes that refused to believe what she saw. Seemingly out of nowhere came a band of horsemen. She couldn't understand why she hadn't spotted them when he had. He reached out and caught her hand and drew her back behind him. She looked concerned when she saw him loosen the gun in his holster. The oncoming horsemen, a dozen of them, were tightly bunched together. When the man who rode at their head flung up his hand, there was a general reining in and a dozen horses were brought to a halt in front of Canavan.

"Posse," he said side-mouthed to Jenny in an effort to assure her that there was nothing to fear. "And he's a lawman. A marshal."

"Oh," Jenny said, and wondered how he knew till

she suddenly spied a silver star pinned to the leader's shirtpocket.

"Morning," the latter said, and added "ma'am" when he saw Jenny peer out at him from behind Canavan. He touched his hat to her. Slacking a bit in the saddle, he asked: "You folks see 'ny strangers around?"

"Yeah," Canavan answered. "Two o' th'm and they were riding double on a plug that didn't look like he had it in him to carry even one o' them."

"That sounds like the pair we're looking for," the marshal said, and murmur ran through the mounted men grouped around him. "Which way were they headed?"

"One o' th'm was named Mack only he isn't headed anywhere. He's layin' in the grass back there a piece," Canavan told him.

The marshal, a rangy, sun-bronzed man of about forty, gave him a curious look and nudged his horse in the indicated direction. When they came abreast of the wagon, the lawman glanced at Willie, then at the two horses that were tied to the tailgate. He pulled up abruptly some twenty feet beyond the wagon, dismounted rather stiffly, a sign of long, unbroken hours in the saddle, and bent over. He straightened up shortly, swung himself up on his horse, wheeled him and came trotting back and reined in at Canavan's side.

"That's one o' th'm, all right," he announced. "Joe Mack. What happened to his sidekick?"

"I wasn't concerned about him," Canavan explained. "Only with Mack who was tryin' to untie my horse and make off with her. The other one hightailed it southward and I didn't try to stop him."

"Think he has too much of a jump on us for us to

catch up wtih him?''

"If he was ridin' a good horse, you wouldn't stand a chance. But that nag he's on couldn't take him too far. So you oughta be able to catch up with him if you keep ridin' and lookin'.''

"Uh-huh,'' the marshal said, settling himself in the saddle. "Oh—if you wanna collect, you'll have to make it to town.''

"Collect what?''

"The reward. There's a hundred bucks a piece offered for those two buzzards, dead or alive.'' He grinned a little at Canavan. "Bet it isn't every day you earn yourself a hundred, is it?'' He turned to the waiting horsemen, ran his eye over them, and finally focusing it on one of them, a thin, rather sad-faced, droopy mustached man, said: "You, Lafe Berry. You look kinda beat. Supposin' you ride back to town with these folks and show them where they c'n find the judge?''

"You goin' after Ellis?''

"'Course.''

"What about my cut o' the reward money when you get him?''

"You'll get it,'' the marshal replied. "Let's go.''

Berry backed his horse away from the others who with the marshal again at their head drummed away to the south. Berry dismounted and dropped the reins at his horse's feet and sauntered forward. He glanced at Dora May, looked at her a second time, then looked at Jenny and remarked: "That's a right pert lookin' young un you've got there, ma'am.''

"Thank you,'' Jenny answered with a pleased smile. "We think so too.''

Berry looked down at the coffeepot and lifted his eyes to Canavan. "C'n you spare some o' that?''

121

"Yeah, sure. Take a minute or so to get it heated up."

The mustached posseman bent over, touched the top of the pot and then the side, came erect again and said simply: "She's fine just the way she is."

Canavan made no response. He emptied his cup into the grass, rinsed it out with water from an oversized canteen, filled it with coffee and handed it to Berry. "What'd those two, Mack and the other feller do? They kill somebody?" he asked.

Berry took a swallow of coffee and wiped his mouth and mustache with the back of his bony hand. "Jumped the sheriff and killed him with his own gun."

"I see."

Berry took another mouthful of coffee, swallowed and said: "That's good coffee. Your missus does a good job o' fixin' it. Most women make it too weak, so that it's more like soup than coffee. And when a man makes a to-do about it they make it so strong, it's the nearest thing to sheep dip."

Jenny had turned and walked off toward the wagon. "Johnny," she called.

Canavan joined her. "Yeah?"

"Think you shoulda said something to the marshal about Dora May and her mother?"

"Don't think it would have meant anything to him. He was interested only in Mack and the one who hightailed it. When we get to see that judge Berry's takin' us to, I'll mention it to him."

"Uh-huh. I was just wondering. Now there's something else. I don't like taking credit for something I didn't do. So if you wanna keep peace in this family, first chance you get you'd better show me how to make coffee the way you do. I like getting compliments. But

122

only when I deserve 'em.''

"Yes, ma'am," Canavan said, saluted her, and trudged back to Berry's side.

"Hope you don't mind, mister," the latter said, "but you were kinda busy. So I helped myself to s'more coffee instead o' waiting to ask if it was all right."

"'Course it was all right."

Berry downed his second cupful, smacked his lips and handed his cup back to Canavan.

"It's quite a piece back to town," he said. "Soon's you're ready to go, supposin' I give you a hand gettin' hitched up?"

"Swell. Gimme a couple o' minutes to get organized. Then we'll hitch up."

Ten minutes later, with Jenny in the driver's seat and Dora May inside the wagon, they were ready to roll. With Canavan astride Willie and riding alongside the wagon, and Berry leading the way, they headed for town. The morning hours went by slowly. The trip itself was quite uneventful with nothing but the plod of the horses' hoofs, the swish of the wheels and the dismal creak of the harness to break the silence of the prairie. The sun was hot and wilting, and it was necessary every so often to stop and let the horses blow themselves.

Then, shortly after noon, Berry who was riding some twenty or thirty feet in advance of the wagon, suddenly twisted around, pointed and yelled: "There she is! Less'n a mile away!"

Half an hour later they followed Berry down a slight decline—at the head of which a signpost that bore the name PIERSON in faded letters lay crookedly in a rock-filled hole—and into a small, sun-drenched and deserted-looking town.

Berry pulled up, wheeled his horse and waited till

123

Canavan and the wagon came up to him. He shifted himself in the saddle, and said: "T'aint more'n a hole in the wall, I know. But it's a pretty decent place to live and the people are right friendly. And that's a heckuva lot more'n I c'n say for a lot o' bigger an' richer towns that I've been in."

"What's the name o' the judge we're gonna see?"

Berry grinned. "Same's the name o' the town," he replied. "The Piersons built it and own most of it. That is, whatever's worth owning. Like the bank, the general store and so on. Wanna tell you about the judge before you take him on. Don't let him scare you any. He looks kinda wild bein' that he's got a big mop o' white hair that nobody ever remembers seein' cut or combed and it stands out on every side of his head. But he's a good man. Square as they come. Maybe a mite straight-laced. Oh, yeah, one thing more about him. He hollers a lot and he's got the voice for it. But he doesn't mean it the way it sounds."

Canavan nodded. "I've met up with others like that. And I don't scare easy. Where'll we find the judge?"

"Down the street a ways," Berry answered, wheeled around and trotted off.

"All right, Jenny," Canavan said.

She jerked the lines and the sweat-coated horses plodded on after Berry. The latter swerved in to the low curb after a bit and pulled up in front of a store whose dirt-smudged window bore nothing on it to distinguish it from several others like it. He dismounted and dropped the reins at his horse's feet, turned and waited till the wagon braked to a stop behind his horse.

Canavan swung down, tied Willie to a front wheel, looked up at Jenny and told her: "Loop the lines around the brake and get down inside with Dora May. I won't be long. Leastways, no longer'n I have to be. But long's you're outta the sun—"

Berry interrupted him. "What d'you say, partner?"

Canavan followed him across the planked walk and into the store. The back door was open and a surprisingly pleasant and refreshing breeze was dancing in. A man with a huge head of unruly white hair was sitting behind a big desk thumbing through some papers. He did not look up.

"Be with you directly," he grunted.

There were several straightbacked chairs backed against the side walls.

"Sit down if you want to."

Berry looked at Canavan who shook his head and said: "Feels good to stand for a change."

"Yeah, does at that. 'Specially after so much ridin' on a skinny backside like mine."

The white-haired man squared back in his chair and looked up.

"Oh," he said when he saw Berry. "What's your problem, Lafe?"

"Haven't got 'ny, Judge," the latter replied, thumbing his sweat-stained hat up from his forehead. "This feller," and he nodded at Canavan, "he's here to collect his hundred bucks for killin' that Joe Mack. Marshal told me to bring him in to you."

"I see," the judge said, eyeing Canavan. "What about Mack's companion?"

"Marshal and the rest o' the men are after him. They'll get him. He," and again he indicated Canavan, "he told the marshall which way to go to catch up with Ellis."

The judge nodded. "Good, Lafe. You can go. I'll take care of our friend here."

Berry patted Canavan on the back, settled his hat on his head and trudged out. As the door closed behind him, the judge who had been ranging an interested and appraising eye over Canavan, said: "Based on the fact that you killed Mack, you must know how to handle your gun as well as yourself. Have you ever considered working for the law?"

"I've done. more than that. I've been a lawman. Texas Ranger."

"Oh? And what are you doing now?"

"On my way to California."

"California, fiddlesticks! What's so wonderful about California?"

Canavan smiled. "Just about everything."

The judge frowned and retorted: "Propaganda. You'll find that out for yourself when you get out there, if you're gullible enough to believe what you hear about it, and go there."

"I've been there," Canavan said quietly.

Pierson's frown deepened, and Canavan, remembering what Lafe Berry had told him, thought to himself: "Here we go. He'll let out a holler that'll lift the roof off."

But to his surprise there was no outburst. Instead the judge asked in a moderate tone:

"Got a family?"

Canavan was glad he hadn't been asked if he were worried.

"Uh-huh," he answered.

"How many children?"

"One."

"How old?"

"Four an' a half."

"You owe it to your family to settle here," Pierson

said authoritatively. "You'll have to look far and wide to find a better place than this to plant your roots and raise your child." When Canavan made no response, the judge added bluntly: "You won't have to go job hunting. I can offer you one right now. The sheriff's job. Pay's good too, forty-five dollars a month. Interested?"

"Nope. Just quit one that paid me more and that woulda been anteed up to sixty-five a month if I'da been willing to stay on."

"Hmm," the judge said, still frowning. "Got a job waiting for you out there?"

"Nope. And I don't want one either. I was raised on a ranch and spent a lot o' years learning about cattle. So when I get to California I'll look for a small place for my own and stick to workin' and buildin' it, and I'll leave it to somebody else to uphold the law."

Pierson gave him a hard, reproachful look, jerked open the middle drawer in the desk and produced a well-filled manila envelope, took some bank notes out of it, counted out ten ten-dollar bills and pushed them across the desk. "Count it. I wouldn't want to cheat you," he said curtly.

"There's a hundred there. I counted it with you." Canavan picked up the bills, folded them in half and put them in his pocket. "Thanks," he said, and turned to go.

"Mean you're going to pass up what might easily prove to be the best opportunity you'll ever be offered?"

"'Fraid I'll have to be the best judge o' what's best for me."

"You're a fool, and an ingrate. Get out!"

Canavan held his tongue. He opened the door and

127

went out, and slammed the door shut. There was instant reaction to it, a yell of protest from inside. He grinned as he walked off. Lafe Berry was waiting for him at the curb.

"Get your dough?" he asked.

"Yeah, sure. But that wasn't all I got."

"What d'you mean?"

"He offered me the sheriff's job and when I turned him down he got put out with me, called me a fool and told me to get out. So I got."

"Only hollering I heard was just now. When you came out."

Canavan grinned again. "I wanted to hear him holler. So I gave him a chance to let loose. I slammed the door."

"Oh," Berry said.

"He kinda surprised me though. 'Specially after what you'd told me to expect out've him. I thought he'd start hollering sooner'n he did. Trouble with him is he's spoiled. Wants to have his own way. Got everybody kowtowing to him, and when somebody who won't knuckle down to him comes along, he acts like a spoiled brat."

"Aw, he ain't that bad."

"You c'n have him, Berry. I don't want him," Canavan said. He pushed his hand into his pocket, fished out a ten-dollar bill and handed it to the mustached posseman who looked at it and at Canavan a little wonderingly. "That's for you in case they don't catch up with that Ellis feller. Wouldn't want you to lose out on your share of the reward money. G'wan, put it in your pocket."

"Well, now," Berry said, pocketing the bill. "That's right nice o' you, partner, and I sure appreciate it. But there wasn't any call for you to do that, y'know."

"I didn't gun down that Joe Mack for the reward," Canavan pointed out. "Anyway, I'm still ahead ninety bucks, and that's fine with me. There some place around where we c'n get a bit to eat?"

"Yeah, sure. Y'see that place down the street on the other side with the sign 'Eat' over the doorway?" Canavan turned and looked in the indicated direction. "It's only a lunchroom. But it's clean and the grub's good, and far's I'm c'ncerned that's all that matters."

"I'll go along with you on that."

"If you wanna get your horses outta the sun before it fries th'm, drive your wagon into the alley 'longside the lunchroom."

"Uh-huh," Canavan said, nodding. "How about you joining us?"

"Thanks. But I've got some things that need tending to. So if it's all the same to you. . ."

"Whatever you say, Berry."

They shook hands gravely and parted, the latter climbing up on his horse, backing him away from the curb and trotting him up the street while Canavan untied Willie, led her around the wagon to the rear and tied her to the tailgate. The Cole horse nearest her promptly looked up interestedly and sought to nuzzle her. She snorted protestingly and the surprised horse hastily moved away from her.

Canavan hauled himself up to the driver's seat and said: "Jenny."

"Yes?"

"Gonna get us something to eat. Think Dora May would like a bite and a glass o' nice, cold milk?"

"I'm sure she would," Jenny answered quickly. "You would, wouldn't you, honey?"

"Oh, yes!" Canavan heard the child answer.

He unwound the lines and released the brake and

drove down the street, the sun-wilted horses plodding along heavily and wearily, and wheeled into the alley next to the lunchroom. It was shady in there. In addition a light breeze was blowing through the alley. The horses whinnied happily. Canavan reached down and took Dora May from Jenny and made his way down with her, and helped Jenny to the ground. Then, emerging from the alley, they filed into the lunchroom.

Nine

"Take your time eating," Canavan instructed Jenny and Dora May. "Wanna kill as much time as we can. Besides giving the horses a chance to cool th'mselves out, the more time we take, the less time the sun'll have at them and at us."

He had already noticed that the back door was open and had already become aware of a pleasant little breeze sifting into the place. So the table he selected stood squarely in the path of the breeze. Dora May was seated between Jenny and Canavan.

"Nice an' comf'table in here, isn't it, honey?" Jenny asked the child.

"Yes, ma'am," the child answered. "It was kinda hot in the wagon."

"Before you get up in it," Canavan told her, "I'll tie back the front an' back curtains so's you c'n get some air in there."

So they took their time ordering, and took even more time eating. It was almost an hour and a half later when they finally pushed back from the table, got up and headed for the door. As they left the lunchroom, with Dora May clinging tightly to Jenny's hand, and turned

131

into the alley, Canavan stopped abruptly and put out a restraining hand. Jenny stopped too and looked questioningly at him. When he motioned for her to back out of the alley and she saw him loosen his gun, she paled a bit but hastily obeyed, pulling Dora May back with her.

Silently Canavan made his way to the front of the wagon, stood motionlessly for a moment with his hand on his gun butt. Then he commanded: "All right. Come outta there or I'll shoot."

There was no answer, no sound either from inside the wagon. Drawing his gun, Canavan sidled along the wagon to within inches of the rear of it. A minute passed, two minutes, three, and then he heard the faint squeak of a floorboard. Guardedly a hatless man poked his head out for a quick look around. Then hoisting one leg over the tailgate he proceeded to climb out. Shifting his gun to his left hand, Canavan suddenly lunged, got a grip on the man's belt, dragged him down to the ground and ignoring the frantic punches that his captive sought to throw at him, slugged him twice and pinned him down by planting his knee on his chest.

"How many more in the wagon?" he demanded.

"One," the man wheezed at him.

Canavan relieved him of his gun, stuck it down inside his pants' belt, and warned him: "One peep outta you and it'll be your last. Understand?"

The man gulped and swallowed hard.

"Now call your sidekick an' tell him to come out so's you c'n get outta here."

Canavan put the fire-blackened muzzle of his gun to the man's temple.

"Now," he hissed at him. "Not loud. Kinda quiet-like."

"Curly, c'mon, willyuh? Wanna get away from

here," Canavan's captive called to his companion.

There was a moment-long delay before the latter answered. "All clear, Zeke?"

"Yeah, sure."

"What was that noise I heard before?"

"Took a header when I was climbin' down."

A man's booted foot and pants leg straddled the tailgate. As before, Canavan reached up. He got a fistful of Curly's shirt and with a sudden yank, dragged him down. He fell heavily, with a body-jarring thud. When Canavan stepped on his right hand, almost grinding it into the ground, Curly cried out. Ignoring it, Canavan bent and tore the gun out of his holster, and with a heave of his shoulder flung it away, far down the alley. Then stepping back and holding his gun on the thwarted pair, he ordered them to empty their pockets. A scant handful of small coins, a key, a pocket knife and a soiled and crumpled-up bandana constituted their personal belongings.

Canavan's lip curled. "Pick up those things," he commanded, "and stand up."

Zeke obeyed without delay. His battered face attested to the power of Canavan's punches. His nose and lips were puffy. A cut under his left eye was oozing blood. Curly, clutching his crushed hand to himself, made no attempt to get up. Canavan grabbed him by his shirt-front and dragged him up. Holstering his gun, Canavan tore open Zeke's shirt. Satisfied that he had not taken anything from the wagon that he might have concealed on his person, Canavan pushed him away and ripped open Curly's shirt. He ran his hands over Curly and again stepped back.

"Let's go," he said simply.

"Wait a minute, Mac," Curly said. "We didn't take

133

anything. So what are you fixin' to do with us?''

"You fellers come from around here?"

"Uh-huh."

Canavan frowned. "I'm gonna give you a break you don't deserve," he said after a moment's thought. "I'll probably be sorry for it and wish I'd brought you into Judge Pierson's instead o' letting you go. G'wan now, get outta here before I change my mind."

The two men needed no urging. They bolted out of the alley and fled up the street.

Jenny, with Dora May almost hidden behind her, was standing on the walk backed against the lunchroom window. She lifted worried eyes to Canavan who smiled at her and said: "They didn't take anything. And rather than get involved with that judge on account o' them, I let th'm go."

· "Oh," she said, and she looked and sounded relieved. "You say anything to that judge about Dora May?"

He shook his head.

"No. Didn't get a chance to. He got sore at me because he offered me the sheriff's job and I turned him down, 'specially after he went to the trouble of telling me what a wonderful place this is to bring up a kid. When I told him we were heading for California, that was all he hadda hear. He gave me the hundred, called me a fool for passing up what he was sure was the best opportunity I'd ever be offered, and told me to get out. So I got."

"Let's get away from here, Johnny."

"I'm willing, believe me. C'mon." He led them back into the alley, had them wait till he had climbed up and tied back the front and rear curtains, took Dora May from Jenny, and put her in the wagon. Then he jumped down and helped Jenny mount to the driver's seat. At his insistence she unwound the lines and released the handbrake. "Just sit tight," he told her. "I'll back you out to the street."

He backed the horses and the wagon out of the alley and into the street, untied Willie and hauled himself up into the saddle.

"All right," he said to Jenny, pulling up alongside the wagon. "Take it easy till we get outta town. Then you c'n ease up a little on the reins."

Just then a man who came striding diagonally across the street, apparently headed for the lunchroom, stopped and said to Canavan: "See you're still here. I hope that means you've been reconsidering my offer."

"Sorry to disappoint you, Judge," Canavan replied. "But the fact that we're still around only means we've just finished having a bite to eat. Now we're heading out."

Judge Pierson frowned. "You, young woman," he said, lifting his gaze to Jenny and addressing her. "Has he told you of what I've offered him?"

"Yeah, sure," Jenny said. "He's told me."

"And that I've pointed out to him that this is an ideal place in which to raise your child?"

"Far's I c'n see, it's anything but ideal. When we were coming outta that lunchroom," and she nodded in its direction," two o' your high-class citizens, two o' the scurviest looking characters I've ever laid eyes on, were up in our wagon looking for something to steal. Let's go, Johnny."

"Just a minute," Pierson commanded, holding up both of his hands. He turned again to Canavan. "Where are they? What have you done with them?"

"They didn't take anything," Canavan answered. "So I let th'm go."

135

"Let them go?" the judge repeated in shocked tones. "Don't you realize that that is encouraging them to commit more crimes? Don't you realize—?"

Jenny had already gotten the wagon under way. Hastily Pierson leaped aside. Canavan guided the mare around him and loped off after Jenny.

"Confound it!" he heard the judge yell in a voice that carried the length of the street and brought several wide-eyed people to doorways of apparently deserted stores to see what had shattered the silence that lay over the town. "I haven't finished with you! Come back here!"

The fleet mare's hoofs drummed rhythmically but only briefly as she overtook the wagon and ranged up alongside. Slowing her to a fast trot to match the wagon horses' pace, Canavan looked at Jenny and grinned at her.

"I don't think the judge likes either one of us now," he told her. "First it was only me for turning him down, and I don't think most people do that to him. Then you upped and talked back to him, and that soured him on you."

"I shoulda kept my big mouth shut. I shoulda left it to you to do the talking for us."

"Any time you've got something to say, you say it."

"No," she insisted. "It isn't the woman's place to do the talking. It's up to the man. I'll remember that next time."

Minutes later they had left the town behind them and were rumbling over the westward road that lay ruler-straight before them. Jenny eased up a bit on the lines. But the horses showed no desire to quicken their pace, and Jenny made no attempt to urge them on.

"Y'know something, Johnny?" she called to

Canavan. "D'you remember that house we passed standing all by its lonesome out in the middle o' nowhere? Remember me sayin' that that was for me? I meant it then and now I mean it even more. Kinda think I've lost my taste for living in town."

"That's being anti-social, y'know. Wanting to get away from other people."

"If that's what that means, what you just said, then I guess that's what I am. Must be I've soured on people and that I've about had my fill o' th'm. All I want now is a place for just us."

"I'm afraid that what you've got now, the wagon, will have to do you for a long time to come."

"That's all right," she responded. "I'm willing to wait till we have something better."

He gave her a curious look. But he did not pursue the matter beyond that point.

Later on that day when they made camp, he handed her a small roll of bills. "Put that away, Jenny. On you. Not in a box where somebody c'n find it. There's ninety bucks outta the hundred that the judge gave me, and Lennart's fifty. Hundred an' forty all told."

"H'm, hundred an' forty, huh?" she said. "That's more'n I've ever had in my life. But how come you're giving it to me to hold?"

"Who else c'n I give it to? Dora May?"

"You're makin' me fell like we're married, giving me your money."

"Mean you don't like the feeling?"

"I didn't say that, did I?"

"No, you didn't. I just wondered. That's why I asked." Then he added gravely: "Y'know before we started out you told me you hope I get so used to having you around, that by the time we hit California I won't wanna let you go, and that I'll wanna keep you around for always."

"Yeah," she said. "I remember saying that."

"If that happens," he continued as gravely as before, "I'm afraid I won't have 'ny alternative. To make you an honest woman I'll have to marry you."

"That'll be real big of you."

"Mean you wouldn't want me to?"

"I ever say anything about me wanting you to marry me?" she demanded.

"No, not that I c'n recall. Leastways, not right out."

"You know I didn't, not right out or any other way. I didn't say it before we started out, or after, and I'm not saying it now either. What's more I never will."

"But supposing I want to?"

"You won't and I don't want you to do me any favors."

She turned away abruptly. He called after her but she stalked off. He followed her briefly with his eyes, finally shook his head, and after a moment or so set about preparing their supper. He was kneeling and bending over the fire shortly after that when someone came up behind him and plucked at his sleeve. When he turned his head he found it was Dora May.

"Want something?"

"No," she replied. "She's crying."

"Huh? Who's crying? Oh, you mean Jenny?"

"Yes," she said, nodding. "Did you make her cry?"

"If I did, I didn't mean to. I don't like to make anyone cry, 'specially Jenny or you." He came erect. "I'll be right back, Dora May. Don't go any closer to the fire."

"I won't."

He patted her gently on the head, hitched up his pants

and headed for the wagon in search of Jenny. He found her shortly, sitting hunched over in the grass a dozen feet beyond the wagon, with her knees drawn up, her arms encircling her head and resting on her knees. She was still sobbing.

He thumbed his hat up from his forehead, knelt down in front of her and sought to take her in his arms. She twisted away from him.

"Go 'way," she told him. "Leave me alone."

"No," he said. "I was only fooling. Teasing you. Thought you knew that."

"No, you weren't," she flared up at him. "You meant it. But that's all right with me. When we get to California, the first town we hit, you c'n drop us off there, Dora May and me. We'll make out by ourselves."

"She's just as much mine as she is yours."

"Doesn't matter. She belongs with me. I can look out for her better than you can."

He eased back on his haunches. "Alluva sudden you've gotten awf'lly touchy, y'know? Now why don't you stop this silly acting up and c'mon back? Dora May got worried when she saw you crying and came an' told me. That's why I came lookin' for you. If you keep her waiting much longer instead o' letting her know right off that you're all right, she'll worry even more. And who knows what kind of ideas kids like her c'n get in their heads?"

When he produced a new bandana and leaned toward her she did not resist. Gently he dried her eyes and her cheeks, even a single teardrop that had come to rest on the very tip of her nose. He pocketed the bandana, got up and helped her to her feet.

But when he put his arms around her and tried to kiss her, she pushed him off, saying: "Don't. I don't want

139

you to kiss me. That's another o' your favors I c'n do without."

He made no response. He simply released her and stepped back from her and followed her back past the wagon. Dora May was standing where he had left her, staring down at the fire, apparently fascinated by the crackling flames. When she heard them coming, she looked around. Jenny stopped and dropped to her knees and held out her arms and the child ran to her and Jenny caught her in her arms and held her tight. Canavan trudged on to the fire and resumed his preparations for supper.

Twenty minutes or so later when they were seated around the fire eating their meal, Dora May and Jenny again sitting together on Canavan's saddle while he sat cross-legged in the grass, Willie suddenly whinnied and both Jenny and Canavan looked up. When Canavan put down his tin plate and got to his feet, Jenny looked troubled.

"Sit tight," he told her, "while I go have a look."

He strode off briskly with his hand resting on the butt of his gun. As he rounded the wagon, Willie whinnied a second time. He moved up to her and patted her gently.

"S'matter, girl?"

This time though, instead of responding to him as she usually did by nuzzling him, she tossed her head, snorted and even shied away from him, and he eyed her wonderingly.

Suddenly he heard a strange voice, a man's voice, and he turned quickly and peered out from behind the back of the wagon. Fortunately it hadn't yet gotten too dark, so he was able to see quite clearly. Standing around the fire were two men, both of them shabbily dressed and stubbly-faced, and both had their hands on their holstered guns as they ranged their gaze around, obviously looking for him. One of them was stocky and barrel-chested, his companion about average in height and build. But the latter, Canavan was quick to notice—and it angered him—was eyeing Jenny with more than just normal interest.

"Asked you something, lady," Canavan heard the stocky man say, "and I'm still waiting for 'n answer. You an' your kid makin' it out here by yourselves and without a man, or—"

"Who are you and what do you want?" Jenny demanded, getting to her feet and moving squarely in front of Dora May.

"That's a saddle she's sittin' on, Jess," the taller man pointed out. "She couldn'ta hauled that over here by herself. Had t'be a man who did it for her. So he must be around here somewhere's. Grab the kid, Jess, just in case he shows up before we're ready to go. Meantime I'll go have a look at their horses an' see if they're any better'n ours."

He moved around the fire, apparently heading for the wagon. He stopped in front of Jenny and smiled. "Well, now! You're even nicer lookin' closer up than I thought. When I think of how lonely I've been at night with nobody 'cept him," and he jerked his head in Jess' direction, "to keep me company, I realize what I've been missing. Gonna be real nice having you around to cheer me up and give me a new interest in life."

"I won't go for that, Wick," Jess said. "We've got enough trouble as it is without addin' any more."

"When I ask your permission to do anything," Wick retorted over his shoulder, "then you c'n speak your piece. But not till than. We're takin' her with us, and if you don't like it, you know what you c'n do."

141

Noiselessly Canavan glided along the side of the wagon and crouched behind the horses that were still standing in the traces. It was Jess who was the first to spot him as he moved a step away from the horses, straightening up at the same time with his gun half-drawn.

"Wick!" Jess yelled, and clawed for his gun.

Canavan's Colt thundered and the stocky man gasped and dropped his gun. Doubling over with his thick arms curled around his middle, he suddenly pitched forward and fell heavily on his face, just missing the fire. Wick then turned toward Canavan and went for his gun only to freeze when he saw the muzzle of Canavan's pistol gaping at him. Slowly, as Canavan advanced toward him, his hand came away from his gun, and he moved backward a couple of steps.

"You scurvy, mangy bum," Canavan raged at him. "So you'd like to have her around to kinda cheer you up, huh?"

He leaped at Wick, battering him, pistol-whipping him in the face and head and forcing him backward under a vicious rain of blows. Blood burst from his cut face and Jenny gasped and turned her back and clutched Dora May to her.

When Wick's legs began to buckle under him and he began to totter drunkenly, Canavan, holstering his gun, grabbed him by his shirtfront and beat him with his free hand. It was only when he ran out of breath and became arm-weary that he stopped slugging Wick and flung him away. Wick fell brokenly. Canavan stood over him for a moment, bent and ripped the gun out of Wick's holster, picked up Jess' gun too, trudged back to the wagon with the two guns and tossed them up on the wide seat.

He was still heaving from his exertions when he rejoined Jenny.

"How d'you like that for gall?" he demanded of her. "That lousy slob! You an' Dora May get up in the wagon. Those two don't do anything to this spot 'cept stink it up. So we'll go find us another."

He followed them back to the wagon, helped Jenny climb up and hauled himself up after her with Dora May in his arms. He put the child on the seat and helped Jenny get down into the body of the wagon and handed her Dora May. Jumping down, he picked up their supper plates and scraped them clean into the fire, causing it to sputter. He flung scooped-up dirt over it, smothering it.

Settling himself on the seat then, he released the brake, flicked the ends of the lines over the horses' heads, stirring them into reluctant movement, and drove westward. Some minutes later he pulled the team to a stop, braked the wagon, and turning, called Jenny.

"Yes?" she answered.

"Found us a swell spot," he told her. "Right next to a stream. I'll water the horses and then fix us something to eat. Wanna gimme Dora May, then I'll help you get down? Oh, better let me have a couple o' lanterns. We're gonna need th'm. It's pretty dark, y'know."

It took him more than forty minutes to get things "set", as he put it. He had just announced that supper was ready when he groaned. "Damnation!"

Jenny looked hard at him. "S'matter?"

"Left my saddle back there."

"Oh? Do you have t'go after it tonight? Can't we pick it up tomorrow morning before we go on our way?"

"Yeah, guess it'll keep over night."

He trudged back to the wagon and returned with two wooden boxes on which Jenny and Dora May perched themselves. Suppertime passed uneventfully. Then it was time for Dora May to be put to bed.

"Bedtime, honey," Jenny told her.

The child got up from her box.

"Goodnight," Dora May repeated.

"I think you c'n do better than that," Jenny said, bent and whispered something to her. "All right?"

"Yes, ma'am."

Dutifully the child came to Canavan and kissed his cheek.

"Thank you," he said. "That was very nice. Now can I kiss you?"

"Yes. If you want to."

"I want to very much." He kissed her cheek. "Good night, Dora May. Happy dreams."

Clinging to Jenny's hand while Canavan trooped after them with one of the lighted lanterns, the child led them to the wagon. Handing the lantern to Jenny, Canavan helped her climb up and watched her maneuver herself over the seat and down into the wagon. Then he followed with Dora May.

He was sitting on one of the boxes within the cast-off rays of the second lantern, staring down into the fire, watching it burn itself out when he heard Jenny call him in a guarded voice.

"Gonna sit up all night?" she asked.

"Be along d'rectly," he told her.

He stamped out the fire and took care of the plates, cups and coffeepot and two frying pans that he had used, and with the lantern swinging from his hand, hoisted himself up into the wagon. He blew out the light and took off his boots, untied the front curtain and let it drop, carefully made his way around the sleeping child, noticing the while that the lantern that he had given Jenny stood on the floor at the rear, with the light in it turned down to its lowest. The back curtain, he saw, had been untied and hung in place, shutting out the night. He undressed himself and eased himself down on the mattress, drew up the cover and turned himself on his side with his back to Jenny.

"Johnny," she whispered, and he turned his head. "Isn't she the cutest thing?"

"Couldn't be any cuter."

"Never thought I could be so crazy about any kid, 'less maybe it was my own. But she does something to me. I have the hardest time of it keepin' myself from hugging an' kissing her every time I look at her."

"She ever say 'nything about her mother? She must miss her."

" 'Course she misses her. And she speaks of her a lot. Mostly when I'm undressing her and getting her ready for bed. When she says her prayers, she always asks God to be good to her mama an' papa because they were always so good to her. And she asks God to be good to us for takin' care of her."

He made no comment. Jenny was silent for a brief time, then she whispered: "When you get mad, you really do a job of it, don't you? The way you went after that man Wick, I thought you were gonna kill him. I didn't know you could get that mad."

"Takes a lot to get me going."

"I mean that much to you, that you woulda killed him for wanting me?"

"Best way I c'n answer that, Jenny, is to tell you something that I wasn't gonna tell you, leastways not just yet. But I guess I might as well."

"I'm listening."

"I had it planned, once I'd finished my business with that Judge Pierson, to have him marry us." He felt her raise up, prop herself up on her elbows, apparently to look hard at him despite her awareness that the deep darkness in the wagon would have made it impossible for her to have seen her own hand in front of her face. "I told you what happened, how he just about kicked me out've his office. So you know why I didn't get to it."

"Wait, now," she commanded. "I wanna get this straight. Y'mean you were really gonna marry me?" she asked in a hushed voice that reflected her disbelief.

"Uh-huh. Really."

"Even though you know you don't have to?"

"Uh-huh," he said again. "Even though."

"You really want to?" she pressed him. "Or is it because you think it'd be the nice thing to do?"

"Look, you tryin' to talk me out of it?"

"I'm not tryin' to do anything, talk you out of it or into it. I just want you to be sure you know what you're doing so you won't be sorry afterwards."

"I'm so sure it's what I want that the next town we hit, whoever's around who has the right to do the job for us, we'll get hitched." Then he added: "Takes two to make a bargain. So you have to be willing to have me. That goes without saying."

She didn't answer. She eased herself down again and lay on her side with her back to him. When he felt her body heave, he knew she was crying. He turned to her, reached out for her and turned her around to him and held her in his arms.

"What's the matter?" he asked her in a whisper. "What are you cryin' for?"

"You're a man. You wouldn't understand."

"Y'mean it's something that only women understand? G'wan, I don't believe that."

"I'm crying because I'm happy. Now tell me that doesn't make sense to you."

"It doesn't. But if it makes sense to you, go ahead an' cry. I'm happy. But if it's all right with you, I won't cry."

"I don't expect you to."

"You finished cryin'?"

"Why?"

"How c'n I kiss you when you're still blubbering?"

"I didn't know you wanted to." She raised her head. "I'm not blubbering now."

Despite the darkness he had no difficulty finding her willing lips with his.

Ten

The days that followed were uneventful. The good weather continued and they were able to make steady and substantial progress. In an effort to use fresh horses, Canavan alternated his original pair with those that he had taken from Mrs. Cole's wagon. The far-flung range seemed to be deserted. There was no sign of life, human or animal, anywhere about them that they could see, and the only sounds that could be heard were of their own making.

But it was an eerie silence that blanketed the land, and while it had no effect on Canavan or little Dora May, it was disquieting to Jenny. She slept poorly, got up a dozen times during the night, and several times when her rising woke Canavan, he found her peering out guardedly from behind a lifted corner of either the back curtain or the front one. Each time she insisted that she had heard something that sounded to her like stealthy bootsteps. Canavan tried to assure her that there was nothing to fear, adding that Willie's sense of hearing was far keener than hers or his, that if there had been anyone about, the mare would have heard it and sounded an alarm. Reluctantly she conceded that she might have imagined it.

Each time he brought her back to bed and she snuggled up close to him. But half an hour later he would feel her ease herself out of his arms and get up again. Every now and then she claimed she had gotten up to see that Dora May was all right. Then during the day he kept watching her and he would find her looking back or standing up, ranging a quick look over the prairie. He made no comment. But he noticed that lack of rest and sleep had begun to take its toll on her; she was sluggish in her movements, short-tempered and appeared to have lost her appetite.

A light, gentle rain began to fall on the night of the fifth day. About midnight when they were asleep, Jenny's exhaustion having finally overcome her, a violent storm burst upon them. The thunder echoed over the hushed range like the roar of distant cannons. The flashes of lightning and the repeated claps of thunder woke the three of them and so unnerved the horses that they struggled frantically to break their tethering lines. The animals milled about in their fright, trampled and kicked one another, and made such a to-do that Canavan was forced to get dressed and go out to them and move about them in an effort to calm them down.

The rain then came pelting down and the accompanying wind tore at the wagon's canvas covering with such fury that it finally succeeded in ripping it off, subjecting Jenny and the child to a severe drenching before Canavan was able to retrieve the canvas and hoist it up over them. Ignoring the driving rain and the howling wind, he managed to secure the canvas.

Wringing wet, he surveyed the interior of the wagon with a critical eye and a sad shake of his head. Twice the light in the lantern that he had lit was blown out, and each time his wet hands made the matches he fished out of his pocket worthless, and he had to scrounge around for dry ones. It was nearly dawn by the time the storm finally abated. The rain gradually stopped and the wind slacked off till it was little more than a breeze.

Jenny and Dora May had taken refuge under the driver's seat and had dozed off. Wearily Canavan stripped off his soggy clothes, dried himself with an old towel that had somehow managed to escape the effects of the rain, donned some old clothes that he had planned to discard, and climbed down from the wagon. The rangeland was a sea of mud, and the wheels of the wagon mired in it. He hunted around till he found a couple of small, flat rocks, uprooted them from the muck, and made a base of them for a fire. He returned to the wagon for a small box that he broke into pieces and set it afire to boil water for coffee. With a couple of cupfuls in his stomach he felt better. Again he returned to the wagon, this time for two lariats that he pressed into service as washlines, looping one end of each around an iron stave that helped support the canvas covering atop the wagon and knotting the other end around the trunk of a droopy-branched tree that stood some twenty feet away. Just about everything, and that included his wet clothes, that he was able to haul out of the wagon without waking Jenny or Dora May was hung out to dry.

At about eight-thirty, a warming, cheerful sun burned off the clouds. Brushing against the two cloth-covered boxes that held Jenny's and Dora May's clothes, he found that while the cloth had received a thorough drenching, the contents of the boxes were quite dry.

It was about the middle of the morning when Jenny awoke. Hearing her move about in the wagon, Canavan brought her a cup of hot coffee.

"Hey," she said when she saw the bright sunshine outside. "What time is it?"

"Must be somewhere's around ten-thirty. Slept all right for a change, huh?"

"And how I did! And Dora May's still pounding her ear. Poor kid, she was scared to death. How bad did we get it?"

"Bad," Canavan replied. "Gonna have to find us a town so's we c'n stock up again. Most of our grub's ruined, water-soaked. Only good thing the storm did for us was fill our water barrel right smack to the top. Outside o' that, it just about put us outta business."

Dora May woke up shortly after that and Jenny interrupted her own getting deessed to put the child in dry clothes. The bedroll and their nightclothes were soon hung on the washline, then Canavan helped the two get down. He stripped off the canvas covering and spread it out in the grass so that the sun could dry it as well as the inside of the wagon.

"Hate to lose a whole day," he told Jenny when the three of them were breakfasting on the last of the buns. Only Dora May made a wry face when she bit into the bun that Jenny handed her and found it was soggy. But when neither of her elders voiced any complaint, she made none either, and ate her bun quietly. "Like I started to say," Canavan began again, "while I hate to lose a whole day, I think we'd better lay over till tomorrow and give the sun a chance to dry us out."

Jenny nodded.

"Besides," he added, "when the ground's so soft, the horses won't find it easy going."

The sun cooperated fully. However at sundown, when Canavan climbed up into the wagon and found the floorboards damp, he hauled out a sheet of canvas and spread it out over the floor as a protective base for the bedroll and the mattress.

Since it had been a long and tiring day for all of them,

everyone was ready to turn in at a rather early hour. The next day proved to be another bright and sunny one and, after an early cup of coffee, they resumed their journey. From time to time throughout the day Canavan ranged ahead of the wagon seeking high ground from which he might spot a town. Unwilling to leave Jenny and Dora May alone for too long, he drummed back every little while to see that they were all right and to give them the assurance of his nearness.

Late in the afternoon when he was about to abandon his efforts, and he was about to wheel around and ride back, Willie whinnied and he promptly twisted around and cast a quick look over the prairie. Coming toward him from about half a mile away was a wagon train with rifle-armed horsemen riding its flanks and half a dozen others at the head of it.

"Comp'ny coming, Jenny!" he called to her as he came loping back.

She pulled back instantly on the lines, halting the wagon, and asked apprehensively: "Trouble?"

He reined in alongside the heaving horses. "Nope. Wagon train headed east," he answered, and turning, pointed to it.

She stood up and followed his pointing finger with her eyes. "Couple o' men coming this way, Johnny," she said.

He wheeled Willie around.

"What d'you suppose they want of us?" she asked.

He offered no opinion. "I'll go meet th'm and find out."

He drummed away to meet the oncoming mounted men. There were two of them, and he came together with them shortly, nodded to them and slacked a little in the saddle. One of the two men said: "When we spotted your wagon, mister, we thought we oughta stop you and warn you that you might be running into trouble."

"Oh? What kind o' trouble? Highbinders?"

"Uh-huh. Gang o' men, about twenty o' th'm, showed up yesterday. The scurviest lookin' crew you ever saw. When they saw the size of our outfit—we've got forty-three wagons and forty-five men and all o' th'm right handy with a gun—they kinda veered off. We've been keepin' a sharp eye out for th'm. But I don't look for them to come around again. They won't wanna tangle with us. We're too strong for th'm. What they go after are small outfits. I kinda think it might be a good idea for you to swing north so's to avoid th'm. Y'know? By the way, I'm Cy Fairly, and this," turning to his companion, "is Mike Cousins. Mike's our scout."

"My name's Canavan, and I sure appreciate you tippin' me off."

"Forget it," Fairly said. "Wish you were goin' our way. Then you could pull your wagon in with ours."

"You pass any towns?"

"Not the last week or so. Fact is, we've been steerin' clear o' th'm and stickin' close to our route. Why d'you ask? Runnin' short o' grub?"

"That storm just about ruined what we had."

"Got enough water?"

"Yeah, sure."

"We might be able to spare you some meat an' flour an' coffee, if they'll help you out. Leastways till you're able to get a real stockin' up."

"I'd be obliged to you for whatever you can spare."

Fairly's train had ground to a halt, and Canavan, lifting a quick look to it could see its people eyeing the lone wagon that stood diagonally opposite it about fifty feet away.

"Suppose you bring your wagon over to our lead wagon?" Fairly suggested.

"Right," Canavan answered.

He parted from the two horsemen, wheeled Willie and loped back to his own wagon. Jenny held her gaze on him as he came riding up to her. He smiled. "Don't look so worried. They don't want anything of us. Instead they wanna help us which proves what kind o' people they are. They offered to fix us up with whatever they c'n spare like meat, flour an' coffee to hold us till we hit a town, and I took th'm up on it."

"Oh," Jenny said.

"Wanna follow me over to their lead wagon?"

" 'Course," she responded.

Trotting the mare across the intervening space to the halted train, Canavan led the way and Jenny followed him, and pulled up when he did. She could see the people aboard the strung-out wagons focusing their eyes on her and she flushed.

Canavan swung down from Willie and was joined by Fairly and Cousins. They talked together briefly, then Canavan followed Cousins away. A handful of women who had already climbed down from their wagons, apparently glad for the opportunity to stretch their legs came sauntering over and stopped just short of Jenny, lifted their eyes to her and smiled. Fairly came up and touched his hat to her.

"Glad to be o' some help to you people, Mrs. Canavan," he said. "Wouldn't you like to get down a minute? Sittin' up there and driving must be kinda tiring after a while."

When he held up his arms to her, she moved across the seat and let him help her climb down.

"Mary," he said over his shoulder, and a slim, graying woman came to his side. "You wanna keep Mrs. Canavan comp'ny while I go see how Mike's takin' care o' her husband?"

"Of course, Cy," was the reply. As Fairly, hitching up his pants and shifting his holstered gun to a more comfortable position, trudged off, his wife asked Jenny: "Where are you headed for, dear? California?"

Before Jenny could answer, the other women crowded forward around Mary Fairly. One of them said: "My, isn't she pretty!"

"She is indeed," Mrs. Fairly said. "Mrs. Canavan, this is Mrs. Macklin," and indicated each of the others with a nod as she introduced them. "Mrs. Halstead, Mrs. Costa and Mrs. McDole."

Jenny exchanged a smile and a murmured, "How d'you do?" with each woman.

She was too busy being lionized by the train women to notice the transfer of foodstuffs from Fairly's wagon to Canavan's. It was only when the two men shook hands that the friendly talk among the uneven circle of women stopped.

"Mind you now," Jenny heard Fairly say to Canavan, "keep a sharp eye out. And don't forget when you get to Sacramento to look up my brother Tom. He'll be only too glad to help you get located."

Canavan nodded and thanked Fairly. Then he turned to Jenny. "Time for us to get rolling."

"Oh," she said, and her voice mirrored her disappointment.

As Canavan helped her climb up to the driver's seat, Mrs. Fairly said: "Sorry we couldn't get a look at your little girl. She must be very lovely."

Jenny, settling herself on the seat and unwinding the lines from around the handbrake, flashed her a smile. "She is."

"She's taking a nap," Canavan added.

"So your wife said."

Jenny had just released the handbrake when

Canavan, astride Willie, looked up at her and nodded. She jerked the reins and the horses plodded away, lurching the wagon into movement behind them. There were cries of "Goodbye" and both responded to them. Then pulling ahead of the wagon, Canavan headed northward. Twisting around and looking up at Jenny, he thought she seemed to be a little puzzled. So he reined in and waited till the wagon came abreast of him and he moved up alongside of it.

But before he could explain why they were changing direction, Jenny said: "We were heading west before, weren't we?"

"Uh-huh, and now we're heading north."

"All right for me to ask why?"

" 'Course. Fairly says there's a gang o' highbinders, bushwhackers, or plain bad men if you like that better, on the loose an' I wanna avoid th'm."

"I see," she said.

"There's hill country northward," he continued, "and Mike Cousins, Fairly's scout, thinks we'll be safer working our way through the hills where we c'n always find cover than down here on the open range where we wouldn't stand a chance if we got jumped."

She was silent for a moment, then she said: "Heard somebody once say that those gangs usu'lly hole up in the hills and—"

"That's right," he said, interrupting her. "They hole up there because they know the law won't go up there after them. Take an army o' men to flush a gang outta the hills and the law never has that many."

"And they come riding down only when they're looking to do some raiding."

"Right again. But being that this gang's down here on the prowl, I figure this is the best time for us to get into the hills and push through and come out the other side

156

while the gang's away and busy. Understand?"

"Yes," she replied. "It'll be getting dark pretty soon. We gonna stop an' make camp, or are we gonna keep going?"

"Keep going long's we can. Closer we get to the hills, the better I'll like it. Then first thing tomorrow morning, the minute it begins to get light, we'll get going again."

He trotted away and Jenny followed him, easing up on the lines in an effort to encourage the horses to quicken their pace. They showed no desire to take advantage of what she offered them. Time passed and the shadows that had already reached out to span the prairie lengthened and deepened. But Canavan ignored them, evidence that he had no intention of stopping till he was forced to. Several times Jenny saw him stand up in the stirrups and quickly look around, then sink down again and ride on. When they came to a thinly grassed incline, the horses slowed their pace, and Jenny flicked the loose ends of the reins over their heads. They responded by manfully toiling upward. When they topped the incline and the ground leveled off, she was surprised to find it barren, hardpacked and strewn with stone and shale that crumbled under the grind of the wheels. But the horses' ironshod hoofs and the iron-rimmed wheels produced an echoing metallic clatter that she was certain could be heard for miles around. Riding some twenty feet in advance of the wagon, Canavan kept looking back at Jenny and the toiling team. A couple of times when he thought the horses were beginning to lag, he beckoned vigorously and again Jenny used the ends of the lines to urge them on. Finally he reined in and waited and when the wagon came up to him, he held up his hand and Jenny promptly pulled back on the lines, halting the heaving horses. It was evening by then and visibility was rapidly decreasing.

"See there?" Canavan asked Jenny, turning and pointing northward.

"What is it?" she wanted to know.

"The hills," he told her patiently.

She looked hard in the direction in which he was pointing. At first she couldn't see anything and was about to say so. Suddenly though she saw it, the barely discernible outline of some low-lying hills. "Oh, yes," she said. "I see them now."

"No more'n about a mile away."

"Yeah, but it's getting so dark, in another couple o' minutes you won't be able to see your hand in front o' your face. Don't tell me you're aimin' to . . ."

"I'd like to give it a try."

There was no answer from Jenny.

"We'll give the horses a couple o' minutes to blow themselves. Then we'll see if they're up to it."

"You're the boss," she said.

He frowned. He hadn't liked the grumpy way in which she'd said that. But rather than call her on it and make a to-do when he realized she was tired and concerned about what could happen to them if they fell into the clutches of the bushwhackers, he remarked: "Haven't heard a peep out've Dora May all afternoon. She all right?"

"Yeah, sure." Leaning down into the body of the wagon, Jenny asked loud enough for him to hear: "You still playing with your doll, honey?" Canavan heard the child's voice, but he couldn't tell what she had said. Jenny squared around. "Dora May says she's doing fine. Kinda hungry though."

"Tell her it won't be long now, no more'n say half 'n hour before we eat. Got some nice cold meat and some cake that I know she's gonna like."

Again Jenny turned, this time to repeat Canavan's words to Dora May. "Next town we come to, we're gonna have to get Dora May a new doll. One she's got now is just about coming apart," she told him.

"We'll get her the best they've got." Straightening up in the saddle and wheeling Willie, he said: "All right, Jenny. Let's go."

Willie responded to Canavan's knee-nudge and trotted away with him. Lightly Jenny slapped the horses with the reins and they snorted protestingly, a sign of their unwillingness to go on. She jerked the lines, perhaps a little harder than she had intended. Reluctantly the horses obeyed her, grumbling deep down in their throats as they moved after Canavan. They started off jerkily, so the wagon swayed and then lurched forward. The big wheels rolled over the rough ground, crushing shale into powder and driving the stones deeper into the dirt. On and on the wagon went with the horses straining in the traces. It was only then that Jenny realized that they were going uphill.

Suddenly from somewhere off in the dark distance beyond them came the startling echoes of gunfire. Grimly Canavan told himself that the raiders had found a victim.

"Johnny!" Jenny cried. "Wasn't that shooting?"

"Sounded like it," he answered over his shoulder.

"Think it coulda been those—what'd you call th'm—bushwhackers?"

"I'm afraid so."

"God, I hope it wasn't the Fairlys that they hit!" she said emotionally. "They're such nice, friendly people."

"I don't think it coulda been them. Their outfit's too big an' too strong for any gang to jump."

"Then it coulda been a smaller one."

"Yeah, that's the kind the bushwhackers go after."

Again Jenny applied the reins, only this time she really lashed the horses. Doubly anxious now to put distance between the raiders who would be returning to their hideout in the hills once they had killed off their victims and had finished looting their wagons, her fears refused to permit any lagging or stopping.

"Go on, go on!" she cried to the horses, and lashed them again.

Wheeling Willie around, Canavan waited, and when the struggling horses came abreast of him, he brought the mare up close to the nearest horse and grabbed the reins.

"Loop the reins around the brake, but easy though," he instructed her. "I'll lead the horses. You get down in the wagon and light one o' the lanterns only keep it down on the floor and don't turn it up any higher'n you have to. Then look around in that stuff that I got from Fairly till you find the meat, cut off some small hunks and you an' Dora May eat. You'll find a knife under the seat. It's in a leather holder. Got that?"

"Yes," she answered. "But what about you?"

"I'll eat later on. Go ahead now. Only hold on when you climb down. Don't want you takin' a spill. And make sure the back curtain's down. Don't want the light to be spotted."

It was just about a minute later when he heard Jenny's voice.

"I'm down, Johnny, and I've lit one o' the lanterns. But you watch y'self, y'hear?"

He didn't answer. He was occupied with the struggling horses as they fought their way up the hills. The upgrade grew steadily steeper the higher they climbed.

Their heaving and panting became louder and several times one of them lost his footing and slipped to his knees. Fortunately though the team continued to forge its way upward.

Twice Canavan halted the horses in order to give them a minute-long breather. And each time that he led them on it was with mixed feelings of hope and misgivings. If they could make it the rest of the way, once they entered the hills, the going would be easier, he told himself. The outline of the hills was gone now, having melted away into the darkness. So he couldn't tell how much farther they had to go. But he was sure it couldn't be very far. Once they reached fairly level ground, he would switch horses, he decided, replacing the exhausted pair with the two that were tied to the tailgate.

It was fifteen minutes later when they came off the upgrade and onto what he judged was a level stretch of ground. Again he halted the hauling horses, unhitched them and led them around the wagon to the rear, untied the fresh team and brought it forward and backed it into the traces and hitched it up, returned to the rear to tie up the waiting pair and hoisted himself up again on Willie's back.

"Johnny!" he heard Jenny call and he turned in the saddle.

"Yeah?"

"Something the matter?"

"Stopped so's I could switch horses. You an' Dora May doin' all right?"

"Yeah, sure. You gonna keep going?"

"Yep. Wanna give the fresh team a chance to earn its keep."

"I'm ready to take over the driving again," Jenny offered.

"No, I think you'd better stay put and take it easy."

"It isn't fair leaving it to you to do everything. You must be pretty well beat as well as starved out. So how about it? How about giving me a chance to earn my keep too?"

"You've done more'n your share already, Jenny. Besides by takin' care o' yourself an' Dora May, you're relievin' me of that worry. So like I said, stay put."

She was silent for a moment. Then she said: "Awf'lly dark out, isn't it? How c'n you see where you're going?"

"Oh, it isn't that bad. Or maybe I'm more used to the darkness than you."

"I suppose so. "You hear 'nymore shooting?"

"Nope. Just that one time."

"Think that's a good sign?"

"Could be that one blast drove off the raiders."

"I sure hope that's what it means."

He turned away, brought Willie up close to the nearest wagon horse, got a good grip on the lines, then gave it a yank and the horses moved with him. On and on they went, and Canavan was aware of a brisk breeze sweeping down upon him. Then suddenly there was no breeze, and he looked up wonderingly. He could see a limited span of the sky but he couldn't see anything on either side of him. Then he noticed that the trail that he had been following had disappeared and that it was even darker than it had been before. Then his leg brushed something that was solid and smooth. He raised his eyes.

Towering high above him and losing itself in the darkness was a canyon wall, and he sensed at once that they were going through a pass. It was a narrow one, just about wide enough for a single wagon to make it through safely. The water barrel that was lashed on to the side of the wagon scraped the wall.

On through the pass they went with Canavan wondering how far it ran and what he would find at the end of it. It was difficult to judge distance in the deep darkness but after a while he guessed that they had spanned a hundred feet of the pass, then still another hundred, and the end of it was not yet in sight. Time and distance continued to fall away behind them. Finally though the wall that had begun to taper off dropped away altogether and they emerged into the open and again Canavan felt the rush of clean, brisk air.

It was lighter now too and when he looked skyward he found a bright moon directly overhead. Rays of silvery light glinted on sun-bleached, white-faced boulders that rose up on both sides of the trail. The ground, he was quick to notice, was fairly level though rough and stony. The grinding wheels and the horses' hoofs produced an echoing clatter. Then they began to go down a gentle slope and quite suddenly there was thinning grass underfoot.

Down and down they went as the grass thickened and muffled the churning wheels and the plodding hoofs. Canavan knew that they had broken out of the hills and had entered a valley.

That their luck had persisted and that it had enabled them to avoid running into the raiders was something to be grateful for, and he was. But he insisted upon believing that if fate had intervened in their behalf and had spared them, it had to be because of Dora May rather than because of them. Fate, he maintained, in an effort to make up to the child for the loss of her parents, would continue to safeguard them if for no other reason than that Dora May had need of them. He wasn't at all certain that Jenny would be willing to accept his belief. But it didn't matter. He believed it and he would continue to believe it.

Eleven

After a couple of days they turned to the southwest
again and then westward. The weeks that followed were
uneventful with each day the same as the one before it.
As though they were crossing a virgin land they saw no
signs whatsoever of others abroad in that vast
prairieland. The weather was good and they took full
advantage of it, putting as much distance between each
day's sunup and sundown as the laboring horses permitted.

"Wonder where we are?" Jenny asked one morning
when she awoke and peered out from behind the front
drop curtain.

"Your guess is as good as mine," Canavan answered
as he kicked off the blanket and reached for his pants.
"All I c'n tell you is what I've been telling you every
time you've asked. We're makin' time and knockin' off
miles every day and that c'n mean only one thing, that
we must be getting closer to California all the time."

"All the same though, wouldn't it be nice to know
where we are, or at least have some idea?"

" 'Course it would. Way I figure it we oughta be in
Colorado, the southern part of it."

"That doesn't tell me much. What comes after Colorado?"

"Utah. Then Nevada and after that California."

"Utah?" she repeated thoughtfully. "Isn't that Mormon country?"

"Uh-huh," he answered, tucking in his shirttail.

"Hey," she said, turning around to him. "How would you like to be a Mormon with a flock o' wives?"

"Thanks but no thanks."

"G'wan," she retorted. "Don't give me that. You could pick yourself different kinds, like a different kind for every day in the week and the nicest lookin' one for Saturdays an' Sundays. What a time you could have!"

"Far as I've been able to find out, man who c'n handle one wife has a full time job on his hands."

"How come they don't have some place where a woman c'n have more'n one husband?"

"Mean you'd like that?"

"I didn't say that. All I did was ask."

"Write a letter to Congress. Maybe somebody there will think the idea's worth trying and he'll get a law passed allowing women to have as many husbands as they like."

"That's what I get for wondering out loud."

"Now you've got me worried."

"I have? What about?"

"You gonna be satisfied with just one husband?"

"Try me and find out."

"Nope," he said with a shake of his head. "I'll wanna know for sure before I marry you."

"Suppose I say 'yes' when the time comes and I change my mind afterward?"

He grinned at her. "Maybe I won't care then. Maybe I'll be glad to get rid of you."

"You ever get to feeling that way about me, Johnny Canavan, and—"

"Yeah?" he teased her. "And what?"

"I don't know," she confessed. "But I think it'd just about finish me. I wouldn't be any good to anybody, me more'n anybody else. Guess all I'd want to do then would be to hide, curl up an' die."

He came across the creaky wagon floor, tiptoeing to avoid disturbing Dora May who was still asleep.

"When I marry you," he said to Jenny in a guarded tone, "it'll be for keeps."

"I wouldn't want it any other way," she said earnestly.

He took her face in his hands and kissed her on the lips. "How about you fixin' breakfast this morning?" he suggested.

"Gee, y'think I c'n do it?"

" 'Course. You've been watchin' me all this past week. Just take your time and you'll do all right," he assured her.

"I'll get dressed right away."

"And I'll go get a fire started."

"I'll want some hot water."

"Gimme five minutes and you c'n have it."

More days passed, as uneventfully as those that had preceded them. Then quite suddenly, and more startlingly than it would have been if it hadn't been for the long spell of silence to which they had become accustomed, the report of gunfire came echoing across the prairie.

Instantly Canavan who was loping along some twenty or thirty feet ahead of the wagon, reined in, wheeled around and dashed back. Promptly Jenny pulled back hard on the lines, halting the wagon team.

"I heard it," she said as Canavan came up to her. The color had already begun to drain out of her face. "Think it means another raid?"

"I'm afraid so," he said. He dismounted and climbed up into the wagon, filled his pockets with shells for his rifle and made his way down again. Hoisting himself up on Willie's back, he told Jenny: "We're gonna head north again. Maybe we c'n circle wide around wherever it is that that shooting's comin' from."

She nodded wordlessly.

He rode northward and Jenny followed him. Mile after mile that was punctuated by distant gunfire slipped away behind them. When he quickened the mare's pace, Jenny lashed the wagon horses and drove faster. There were more and more bursts of gunfire that carried across the range, and Canavan wore a grim look as he continued to lead the way. From time to time he stood up in the stirrups and peered intently in a westward and then southwestward direction. He felt a little less worried when he failed to spot anything. But just as he sank down in the saddle after a last look there was the grass-muffled thumping beat of horses' hoofs and he spied four mounted men coming toward them at a swift gallop from about half a mile away. He pulled up at one but beckoned Jenny on and the wagon came abreast of him.

"Four men comin' this way," he said. "Now don't panic. I think I c'n hold them off. Keep headin' north and don't stop or even slow down. Y'hear? I'll follow you soon's I can. Just watch yourself and don't go worryin' about me. I think you know I c'n take care o' myself. Go ahead, Jenny."

"I'm goin'," she answered. "Only be careful, Johnny."

"I'm not lookin' to die just yet," he said lightly.

She flicked the reins over the horses' backs and they responded and the wagon lumbered away. Yanking his rifle out of the boot, he hand-held it across the saddle as he followed Jenny at a trot. The wagon, in full flight now, soon got far ahead of him and as he watched it continue to lengthen the gap between them, he nodded approvingly.

Looking back over his shoulder he watched the oncoming horsemen narrow the distance between him and themselves. He held his hard eyes on the man who rode in advance of his companions and when he suddenly raised his rifle and fired, the man toppled off his horse and crashed to the ground. He fired a second time and his bullet struck squarely, sending one of the others' horses plunging to his knees and catapulting his rider over his head. Obviously stunned, the man lay motionlessly in the grass. The wounded horse threshed about wildly for a minute or so, then his body seemed to relax and then, like the man who had been riding him, he too lay still.

Easing himself around, Canavan sent the fleet mare loping away. When he looked back the two surviving horsemen were lashing their mounts as they sought to overtake him. Both men fired at him, but their shots fell far short of him. Reining in briefly and waiting for his pursuers to come a little closer, he fired again and his eyes gleamed when he saw a third man sag brokenly in the saddle and fall off his horse. The fourth man fired again at Canavan but this time his bullet went wide. Bringing his horse to a sliding stop, he wheeled around, and abandoning his felled companions and further pursuit, rode off in a westerly direction. Reloading his rifle and shoving it down in the boot, Canavan drummed away after Jenny.

He overtook her after a spirited run and ranged up alongside the wagon, slowing Willie at the same time.

"You all right?" she asked him, pulling back a little on the lines and slowing the team to match the mare's pace.

"Yeah, sure," he replied. "Don't have to worry any about those four. I got two o' th'm, spilled the third one, and saw the fourth man turn around and ride off."

She looked relieved. "We still gonna keep headin' north?"

"Yeah, sure. That feller that turned tail will tell the rest o' the gang and if they decide to come after us, I wanna give th'm as hard a time to catch up with us as I can."

"Uh-huh. You gonna lead the way again like before, or d'you want me to go on ahead?"

"Go on same's you were. I'll follow you only I'll kinda hang back a little and keep an eye out for uninvited company."

She smiled a bit and drove on. Canavan did not ride after her right away. Instead he sat Willie motionlessly for a time, ignoring her whinnying, a sign of her eagerness to rejoin the wagon horses, and looked southward and then shifting his gaze, looked westward.

A couple of times he stood up in the stirrups for an even better view of the range. When he seemed satisfied that there was no sign of renewed pursuit, he sank down in the saddle, swung Willie around and trotted her northward. The mare wanted to run; twice she sought to lengthen her stride. Each time Canavan checked her and ignoring her snorting, forced her to trot.

When he spotted the wagon idling a hundred yards or so ahead of him, Canavan gave the mare her head and she bounded away with him. He pulled her up short when they came abreast of Jenny.

"Horses were beginning to slow themselves," she explained to Canavan. "So I figured I oughta give th'm a breather."

"Uh-huh," he said.

Ten minutes later the horses appeared to be sufficiently rested and ready to go on again. When the wagon lurched after them, Canavan wheeled into position some fifteen feet behind it. Time passed slowly. Eventually the day wore away. But because he was unwilling to chance being overtaken while it was still light, Canavan instructed Jenny to keep going. It was only when darkness forced them to stop that he conceded and called to Jenny to pull up.

Without a fire, supper was limited to some cold meat. When Canavan announced his intention to stay up, Jenny quickly informed him that she wouldn't turn in either. It was only when he insisted that she go to bed and promised to wake her at once if he heard anything that she finally agreed to lie down. She wouldn't be able to sleep, she maintained, knowing that he was still awake. So, fully clothed except for her shoes, she stretched out on the mattress. But she was tired and despite her insistence that she would only doze, she fell into a tight sleep.

Looking in on her a half an hour after he had helped her climb up into the wagon, Canavan gently drew up the blanket around her, saw to it too that Dora May was well covered up, hauled out a heavy jacket and quietly left the wagon.

There was a rapidly stiffening breeze blowing, and it was a cold one. He quickly donned the jacket and buttoned it up, whipped up the collar around his neck, and, with his rifle slung over his shoulder, he kept watch.

After a while he decided to switch horses, so he replaced the tired team with the pair of fresh ones, backed them into the traces and hitched them up. He did not unsaddle Willie. She too would be ready to move at a moment's notice.

He sauntered about, stopping every little while and standing motionlessly, listening for sounds of horses and men. But he heard nothing except the usual night sounds.

At the first sign of light in the drab dawn sky he climbed up into the wagon and reluctantly shook Jenny awake. At his insistence, because the air was damp and raw, Jenny wrapped their blanket around herself before she took her place on the seat and prepared to drive off. When they got under way again and he led her in a southwesterly direction, she did not question the wisdom of returning to their orignal route. His judgment had been faultless, so she saw no reason to doubt it now. Obviously he was satisfied that they had left the raiders behind them. So she was satisfied too.

At about eight, when the sun completed the job of burning off the dampness and the chill, she shed the blanket, bunched it up and half-turning, dropped it behind and below the seat. He had taken off his heavy jacket half an hour before and had tossed it up to her. Now the blanket lay on top of the jacket. At nine Dora May awoke and Jenny called to him. Wheeling around, he came trotting back to Jenny's side.

"Any chance o' getting a cup o' coffee?" she asked him.

"Yeah, I think so. What d'you hear from Dora May?"

"So far, only that she's awake."

"How d'you suppose some hot cakes, bacon an' coffee'll sound to her?" he asked gravely.

"I don't think she'll mind if I answer for her. Sounds swell. I didn't do any washin' up, y'know. And I'm sure Dora May's face and hands c'n do with some soap an' water."

"Gimme a little time to get a fire going. Five minutes after that you c'n have your hot water."

"I was gonna fix breakfast this morning if you thought we could have a fire."

"And I was gonna let you. But you've got other things to do. So I'll let you off this time and do the fixin' myself."

"You're an angel, Johnny. Is it any wonder that I love you?"

He grinned at her. "G'wan. Don't gimme any o' that. It's the Irish who are supposed to dish out the mullarkey. Not the Polish."

"Maybe some o' the Irish in you has rubbed off on me," she answered. She braked the wagon and looped the reins around the brake, turned and eased herself over the seat and disappeared inside the wagon.

He was still grinning when he dismounted and tied Willie to one of the wagon's front wheels. Then he set about finding a suitable spot for a fire.

It was shortly after ten when they resumed their journey. Again a great silence hung over the open country. Then just before the sun moved into position directly overhead with its unspoken announcement that it was noon, they turned westward. It was just before two o'clock when they made their second stop. Their midday meal which consisted of cold meat took but fifteen minutes, and they pushed on again. It was about four when the wagon horses began to labor and Jenny promptly called Canavan's attention to it. Dismounting, he unhitched them and substituted a rested team.

As he stepped up to the waiting mare and prepared to mount her, Jenny who had been looking on quietly, asked him: "Switching horses this late in the day mean you're gonna keep going for a while after it gets dark?"

"That's the general idea," he replied. "You add up the extra miles we knock off every day after sundown and you'll be surprised to find how many days' travelling time they come to. Let's go, Jenny."

It was late afternoon and then dusk and still Canavan kept pressing on, challenging the oncoming darkness and daring the night to deprive him of those extra miles he sought to put behind them. Loping away in search of some high ground and leaving it to Jenny to catch up to him, he rode up a grassy incline, halted Willie at its very crest and gave her an opportunity to blow herself while he ranged a long look over the prairie.

Despite the cushioning and muffling grass that carpeted the prairie he was able to make out the pounding beat of massed hoofs and the churning roll of many wagon wheels. Movement to the east attracted his attention and as he leveled his gaze at it a wagon train that was still on the move in spite of the approaching nightfall came into view. It was a good-sized train with its wagons drawn up in a double row with mounted men of whom he could see some six or seven riding its flanks.

"Feller who's bossing that outfit knows his business," he thought to himself. "With outriders to hold off raiders and the wagons doubled up and all set to circle up at a minute's notice, the gang that tries to jump that train will find it's bitten off a helluva bigger bite than it can chew. Damned little chance for anybody to break through without being blasted to hell an' gone."

174

The outriders ranged up and down the entire line of wagons, apparently urging lagging drivers to speed up and close any gaps that existed between them and the wagons directly ahead of them. The train came closer all the time, and as Canavan watched, the lead wagons came abreast of him and rolled past him.

He swung Willie around and rode down the slope and trotted her back to meet Jenny. Suddenly his keen ears caught the drum of approaching horses and he jerked his head and around instantly and looked northward. He sucked in his breath and stared with wide, troubled eyes when he spotted a band of tightly bunched together horsemen heading in Jenny's direction at a swift gallop. He sent Willie racing to meet her, and when he came close enough to her, he pointed northward.

"Raiders!" he shouted. "head for that wagon train!"

As proof that she understood and that she had no intention of panicking, she swerved southward. She drove the horses toward the train at a furious though somewhat uneven gallop with the wagon lurching from side to side when its wheels rolled over half-buried rocks. Yanking out his rifle, Canavan flung two shots into the raider's ranks, causing one man to sag brokenly in the saddle and plunging another's horse to the ground.

The wounded animal cried out in pain and rolled over a couple of times from side to side and finally rolled over his thrown rider, crushing him under him. Again Canavan pegged two shots at the raiders. He missed with one shot, but steadying himself succeeded in targeting a victim for his next shot, tumbling a man off his mount.

The riderless horse skidded to a rather uncertain stop,

and turning, collided head-on with another mounted man. The two horses and the horseman went down in a tangle of threshing legs and flashing hoofs. Again Canavan fired, but again he missed. Shoving his rifle down into the boot, he drew his Colt and snapped a couple of shots at the raiders, then without pausing to see the effect of his fire, he dashed after Jenny.

As he neared the train he saw that it had ground to a halt, and saw too that several of the outriders as well as men on foot were pouring gunfire into the already thinned out raiders' ranks. Overtaking Jenny, he pulled up when she did after giving him a couple of anxious moments when he was afraid she was going to pile into one of the halted wagons. Fortunately she was able to stop in time to avoid crashing into it.

Breathing a deep sigh of relief, he dismounted. Horsemen from the train flashed past him and he followed them with his eyes, lifted his gaze beyond them and saw four raiders, apparently the only survivors of the band, wheel around and ride off. Shot down men and horses were strewn about, some of them lying in grotesque positions. A fatally wounded horse, obviously already overtaken by death, lay on its side with its legs thrusting straight out and stiffening. A dozen feet away was a raider who was down on his knees with his body hunched over and his bowed head nudging the ground, his hands hanging limply at his sides, but with his backside higher than the rest of him.

Just as Canavan was about to shift his gaze, the man slumped over and sprawled out on his back.

Armed riflemen and returning mounted men converged upon Jenny and Canavan. She turned and lifted Dora May onto the seat with her. When willing hands reached up for them, Jenny passed the child to a stalwart, bearded man who handed her to Canavan.

Then Jenny was helped down from the wagon and she held out her arms to Dora May. The child leaned toward her and Jenny took her from Canavan and held her tight.

A tall, rangy man with a deeply lined and weatherbeaten face and gray hair showing in his sideburns pushed through the other men to Jenny's side, chucked Dora May under the chin, and asked Jenny: "You all right, ma'am?"

She flashed him a smile. "Yes, thank you."

"Good." He turned to Canavan. "That was a real close one, mister."

"Too close," Canavan replied wryly. "We'da been goners if you people hadn'ta come along when you did."

The man smiled and said: "That's one gang o' bushwhackers less for us to worry about. But they weren't as smart as they shoulda been, followin' you right down into the muzzles of our guns. 'Course it could be that they didn't see us till it was too late for them to pull up and turn tail. I'm wagon master. Name's Tom Bonner."

"Mine's Canavan."

The two men gripped hands.

"You headin' for California?" Bonner asked. "If you are, and if you an' your missus have had enough of tryin' to make it across the prairie by yourselves and you'd like the protection we c'n give you, pull your wagon into line wherever you find an empty space. Oh, it'll cost you twenty-five bucks to join up with us."

"Fair enough," Canavan acknowledged.

"Forgot to say that that's what it'll cost you if you've got your own grub. If you haven't—"

"Haven't got enough left to make it worth talking about."

"Then it'll cost you more. But that part o' the deal we c'n figure out later on. We'll keep tabs an' let you know later on, say when we're nearing California, what it comes to and you c'n square up before you leave us."

"Want the twenty-five now?"

Bonner grinned. "Uh-huh. It's not that I don't trust you or any o' my other people. I do. It's just that I find it's a heckuva lot easier on me doing a cash-in-advance business. Saves me from burning the midnight oil, keepin' books and makin' out bills and handing 'em out and then having to hound people to pay me what they owe me. Keep just one little book that tells me how much I've taken in and how much I've laid out. So I'll take my dough now."

Canavan dug in his pants pocket and hauled out a fistful of crumpled bills. From among them he drew out a couple of tens and a signle five-dollar bill, and started to smooth them out only to have the wagon master stop him.

"They're fine just the way they are, Canavan. I don't care what they look like or what shape they're in. What's more, I'll take a whole barrelful just like yours and I'll be only too glad to do the smoothing out myself and it won't matter even one little bit how long it takes me."

Canavan handed him the bills and Bonner stuffed them in his pocket.

"Now suppose you pull your wagon into line so's we c'n move on? Don't wanna make camp where there are a lot o' dead men and horses layin' around. They don't smell too good and they don't add anything to the scenery. Besides I don't think our women an' kids would like lookin' at them."

Canavan nodded and turned away.

"When we get circled up," Bonner added and

Canavan looked back at him over his shoulder, "bring your family over to my wagon for supper. I'll tell the cook to fix some extra."

As Canavan squared around again he collided with the big bearded man who was obviously waiting for him for he had moved in front of him deliberately, blocking his path. Both put out their hands, Canavan doing it instinctively, to hold off the other.

"Only keep you a minute, partner," the big man said. "But I heard you say your names Canavan. You come from Texas, say around Amarillo way?"

"That's right. Why? Why d'you ask?"

"Last I heard from my brother, he was still riding for a big outfit around Amarillo and the man who owned it was named Canavan."

"John Canavan's my father."

"And Arlie Watts is my brother."

"I know Arlie. Haven't seen him though in some time now."

"That makes two of us. I'm Steve Watts."

"And I was named for my father."

The bearded man laughed and thrust out his big right hand. Canavan shook it.

"Small world, huh?" Watts asked, chuckling and pumping Canavan's hand vigorously. "Arlie swears by your old man, Canavan. Fact is, he treats Arlie like he's one o' the family, like he's one o' his sons. First chance I get, I'll get off a letter to Arlie so's he can tell your folks who I met up with."

"Fine," Canavan said, nodding. "You do that."

"Oh, something that Arlie wrote in one o' his letters just came to me. One o' you Canavans joined the Rangers, right?"

"Right. And I was the one. But that was a long time ago."

"I'd sure like having you for a neighbor, Canavan. How about you pullin' your wagon into line next to mine?"

"Wanna lead the way?"

Minutes after Canavan had driven his wagon into the space that the burly Watts had led him to, the train ground forward again. Half a mile farther westward the order to pull up and circle up was relayed down the line. While Jenny and Dora May were in the wagon getting cleaned up, Canavan idled, leaned back against the right front wheel. It was there that Tom Bonner found him when he came riding around.

The wagon master reined in front of him. "See you've found a place for yourself," he said.

"Steve Watts led me to it. And I want to ask you something, Bonner."

"Ask away."

"Somebody once told me that in the eyes o' the law wagon masters have just about the same authority that ship captains do. That right?"

"Whoever told you that told you right."

"You ever marry any people?"

"Yeah, sure. Any number o' times. But who are you askin' for?"

"Being that I don't know any o' the people in the train 'cept Watts and being that he's been married for more'n fifteen years now, it figures that I must be askin' for me, doesn't it?"

Bonner looked hard at him. "Y'mean you and . . .?"

Canavan nodded. "That's right. Jenny an' me. You have to know how come we aren't married?"

"Nope," Bonner said evenly. "None o' my business. All I ask o' my people and that includes you now is that they keep the peace an' do their best to get along with the others. When d'you want me to do it?"

"Some time tonight. When there's nobody around. I don't want a crowd around to embarrass Jenny."

"Everybody usu'lly turns in around ten o'clock. That is, everybody 'cept those who are due to stand guard. That's something you'll have to do too, Canavan, along with the others. But that only means about once every six nights."

Canavan nodded again. "That's all right. Just lemme know when it's my turn and I'll be ready."

"Know where my wagon is?"

"Lead wagon, I suppose, huh?"

"No, that's the supply wagon. Mine's the one behind it. Supper oughta be ready in about half 'n hour."

"We'll be there," Canavan told him, "and we'll bring our appetites."

Bonner grinned and responded: "Lee Sing's a good cook. If you don't act like you're enjoying his cooking, you'll make him very unhappy."

"I c'n tell right now that we're gonna like everything he dishes out to us."

"That's the kind o' spirit that makes friends," the wagon master said, backed his horse and trotted him away.

It was some twenty minutes later when Jenny announced that Dora May and she were ready to be helped down from the wagon. Quickly Canavan responded, climbing up first to carry down Dora May, then he helped Jenny get down. While he looked on gravely, Jenny and Dora May, hand-in-hand, stood before him.

"Well?" Jenny wanted to know. "How d'we look?"

"Fine," he replied. "I don't usu'lly go in for bragging, but I think my womenfolks are just about the best lookin' anywhere. That a new dress you've got on, Jenny?"

"Uh-huh. One I've been saving for a special time.

Not that tonight's anything different from any other night. But I put it on anyway."

"Looks fine."

With Dora May walking between them, they headed for Bonner's wagon. Tom Bonner was waiting for them. Lee Sing, a short, pudgy, round-faced Chinaman, greeted them with a broad, toothy smile and even added a bow to Dora May. He made a to-do out of helping the child seat herself on a towel-covered box.

Bonner who stood by quietly looking on smiled at Jenny. "Can't let Lee outdo me. Don't remember the last time I had such lovely ladies at my table. Pleasure to have you here, ma'am." Turning to Dora May, he added: "You too, little lady."

Supper was a huge success. Lee Sing was generously complimented and beamed. When it was over and Jenny arose, Dora May did too.

"Thank you, Mr. Bonner," Jenny said. "And thank you again, Lee Sing."

"Our pleasure, ma'am," Bonner acknowledged. Then turning to Canavan who had just gotten to his feet, he said: "I'll be looking for you at ten."

"Right," Canavan answered.

As they headed back to their own wagon, Canavan remarked: "Be dark by the time you get Dora May tucked in."

Instead of answering, Jenny asked: "What are you and that Bonner man going to do at ten?"

"You're included in that too."

"That's nice. Then it should be all right for me to ask what we're going to do at ten, shouldn't it?"

He smiled, and leaning toward her, told her in a guarded whisper: "We're going to get married."

She stopped in her tracks and looked hard at him.

"You—you really want that?"

" 'Course I do. You asked me that once before and I told you the same thing then. Remember?"

"Yes. But that was then and this is now."

"Doesn't matter. I still feel the same way. That's why I asked Bonner if he could do the job for us. When he said he could and I told him we wanted it done when there wasn't anybody around, he set it for ten because that's when everybody's us'ully bedded down."

"I see."

"You don't sound very happy about it."

"You've never told me anything about your folks. They must be rich and important, judging by what that man, that Steve Watts said. Anyway, it got me to thinking. I'm a nobody and I come from very ordinary people. So I haven't got a thing to offer you. Why even this dress I'm wearing and the shoes I'm standing in, you bought them for me. And that goes for just about everything else I've got. If you hadn'ta bought them, I just wouldn't have a thing. What d'you want me for, Johnny? You could do lots better for yourself."

"I want you because I love you," he told her quietly. "And I know you love me. And if all you've got to offer me is you, I'll still be doing all right for myself. So being that I'm satisfied, you should be satisfied too."

"I don't like to keep asking you this, but are you sure? I don't want you to be sorry afterwards."

"I never felt so sure about anything in my life."

"All right, Johnny. I want to marry you more than anything in the world."

As he straightened up, Dora May looked up at her. "You crying, Jenny?" the girl asked.

"Yes, honey. I'm crying because I'm happy."

"Oh," the child said, obviously satisfied and relieved. She turned to Canavan, lifted her eyes to him. "Don't you want to hold my hand like Jenny does when

183

we're walking?''

He looked down at her. Suddenly he knelt down.

''It's late, you know, and you must be tired,'' he told her, taking her hand in both of his. ''Wouldn't you like to ride the rest of the way on my shoulders?''

''Oh, I'd like that!''

''Then up you go!''

He lifted her, settled her comfortably across his broad shoulders and, holding her hands in his, turned to Jenny. ''All right?''

''Yes,'' she responded brightly.

Then, with her arm through his and Dora May laughing when he jounced her up and down, they marched on.

BORDER RIDERS

ROBERT STEELMAN

Lieutenant David Pine rode into his hometown after six years' absence to find that things had changed. A shadow of fear hung over the town—fear of the ruthless killer, General Pancho Villa.

When Villa's hell-bent gang stormed in, Pine witnessed a slaughter that sent him thundering across the border after the murderers, and into the hands of the desperado Paco Mora. To save his life, David Pine, U.S. Army, was forced to fight side by side with the most vicious outlaws in history!

Before it was over, Pine would be branded a criminal. He'd spill blood on both sides of the border, as he rode a cruel trail that could lead either to freedom—or a noose!

WESTERN

0-8439- 2059-9

$2.25

THE OTHER SIDE OF THE CANYON

ROMER ZANE GREY

THE OTHER SIDE OF THE CANYON marks the return to print of one of Zane Grey's strongest characters, Laramie Nelson, first introduced in Grey's novel RAIDERS OF SPANISH PEAKS. Laramie was a seasoned Indian fighter, an incomparable tracker, and one of the deadliest gunhands the West had ever known.

In these stories, Romer Zane Grey, son of the master storyteller, continues Laramie's adventures as he takes on a gang of train robbers, a gold thief, and a sharp-shooting woman wanted for murder!

WESTERN
0-8439
2041-6
$2.75

GUN TROUBLE IN TONTO BASIN

ROMER ZANE GREY

Gun Trouble In Tonto Basin signals the reappearance of Arizona Ames, the title character of one of Zane Grey's most memorable novels. Young Rich Ames came to lead the life of a range drifter after he participated in a gunfight that left two men dead. Ames' skill earned him a reputation as one of the fastest guns in the West.

In these splendid stories, Arizona Ames comes home to find his range and his family haunted by the shadow of a terror they dare not name!

WESTERN
0-8439-2098-X
$2.75

THE RIDER OF DISTANT TRAILS

ROMER ZANE GREY

The Rider Of Distant Trails marks the return to print of one of Zane Grey's most memorable characters, Buck Duane, first introduced in Grey's novel *Lone Star Ranger*. Forced to turn outlaw as a young man, Buck later teamed up with Captain Jim MacNelly of the Texas Rangers and proved himself to be the Ranger's deadliest gun.

In these stories, Romer Zane Grey, son of the master storyteller, continues Buck's adventures in Texas and as he takes on outlaws who are terrorizing ranches and towns in this tough cattle country!

WESTERN
0-8439-2082-3
$2.75